WINNING
YOU
OVER

PANDORA PIERCE

WINNING YOU OVER
Copyright © Pandora Pierce, 2023

Cover design: MoorBooks Design
Chapter header designs: Fred Kroner of Stardust Book Services
Formatting: Rae Davennor of Stardust Book Services
Book Coach: Cathy Yardley
Book Coach: Rachel May of Golden May Editing
Book Coach: Heart Full of Ink
Copy Editor: Jessica Snyder Edits

First Edition: February 2023

ISBN: 9781960239020 (paperback)
ISBN: 9781960239006 (ebook)

Published by Pandora Pierce LLC

https://pandorapierce.com/

Also by Pandora Pierce

Divine Duelist Series
Playing with Lightning

Connect with Pandora Pierce

Discord: https://discord.gg/jAZzTrSc5z
Facebook: https://www.facebook.com/pandorapierceauthor
Instagram: https://www.instagram.com/pandorapierceauthor/
TikTok: https://www.tiktok.com/@pandorapierceauthor
Twitch: https://www.twitch.tv/pandorapierceauthor
Website: https://pandorapierce.com/
YouTube: https://www.youtube.com/@pandorapierceauthor

Table of Contents

Chapter 1 . . . 1

Chapter 2 . . . 14

Chapter 3 . . . 36

Chapter 4 . . . 51

Chapter 5 . . . 65

Chapter 6 . . . 79

Chapter 7 . . . 92

Chapter 8 . . . 100

Epilogue . . . 113

CHAPTER 1 – CHANTARA

The best part about watching Divine Duelist on the Shimmering Isles was being close enough to have Eros, the god of love, flying within inches of me in all his shirtless glory. Well, a magical construct of him, but it was as close as I'd ever get to the real deal. I leaned back in the coliseum seat, enjoying the colorful night sky as the aurora fueled the cards in the duel, making them come to life with shimmering abs a woman like me could appreciate.

Fans and duelists alike had flocked here in droves ten years ago when the TV station created a way to make a card game appear lifelike. The station broadcast every duel live, making it one of the most popular sports in Nisia. The duelists were celebrities and the rest of us made our livings by supporting them on the island purchased for the game.

Sadly, the TV station didn't trust its famous duelists' hair to newbie hairstylists, not even a stylish water nymph like me. So, I started with the lower-ranked duelists and was working my way up. Or at least, that was the plan. At the moment, Leena was my only client.

I'd been saving the seat next to me, hoping an eager duelist would want a front-row seat to this match, but so far only fans had asked if they could sit there. I loved doing their hair too, but they wouldn't gain me the fame I needed to get promoted. Only duelists on prime-time TV could do that. Unfortunately, with the duel half over, I was starting to lose hope. I moved my bag off the seat so anyone could sit there. No point being a jerk if I didn't have to be.

The scent of grapes filled the air as the Dionysus team's grapevines card darted across the field, tangling around Eros' leg and yanking him down. I winced as the gorgeous god shattered against the ground. The light that had been fueling his card returned to the night sky, honoring the card's sacrifice.

A muscular guy armed to the teeth sidled up next to me, taking the open seat. He was so focused on the game he didn't even acknowledge me when I tried to say hello. He just stared straight ahead, scowling, like he might attack one of the duelists if they made a bad move. I clenched my bag, my blue skin glowing in the aurora's light.

With a deck box on his belt and a tattoo of crossed swords on his wrist, he appeared to be a duelist. Probably an Ares one. They were often fighters in real life too and he certainly looked the part.

I ran through the list of duelists I knew but couldn't place him. I was here to find new clients, but I'd rather stay away from anyone dangerous. No matter how much his shaggy brown hair screamed to be cut.

"Need something?" His voice was gruff as he glanced sideways at me with unnerving red eyes. Those had to be contacts, right? No, they were too piercing to be fake. I wished I could see them without that mess of hair he was hiding behind.

He made an annoyed noise that reminded me I hadn't answered him yet. Getting distracted by sexy guys was a problem I should work on.

"Sorry." I blushed, a bit of steam curling off my cheeks. "I was just picturing different hairstyles on you."

"What?" His lips twitched, like he wanted to smile, but that would be too sweet for a man like him.

"I'm Chantara, an up-and-coming hairstylist for the stars." I held out my hand, not wanting to judge him before even getting to know him. You never know, he could be famous next week if the fans took a liking to him. He was attractive, in a kind of terrifying way.

"Damon." He made a point not to shake my hand, turning his attention back to the duel.

Fine then. I dropped my hand, no longer wanting to act friendly. His eyes narrowed as Leena's partner used an Aphrodite's seduction girdle card to lure the Dionysus team's nymphs to his side. As if we were that easy to lure. I harrumphed, choosing to cheer for Leena instead.

I used my magic to spell Leena's name in water above my head, big enough for her to see from the field.

"You've got this, Leena!" I threw my hands up, turning the watery letters so they'd sparkle with the pink light of the aurora. "Don't let the Drunken Duelists beat you!"

I actually thought the Dionysus team, nicknamed the Drunken Duelists because they spent half the game drinking wine, were a ton of fun to watch, but I couldn't cheer for them when Leena was their opponent. She'd been my first friend here, a duelist willing to let a no-name nymph style her hair however I wanted. It had given me a confidence boost for sure and I'd cherished our friendship ever since.

Which was why I always took it upon myself to cheer extra loud for her since nobody else ever did. They were too focused on her obnoxiously attractive teammate, Kai. Slimy jerks weren't my type, no matter how pretty they were. I preferred somebody honest, somebody who respected me.

I used more water magic, letting it spin through the air, threading around the other fans to encourage them to cheer too. Everyone's faces lit up, their gazes following the flow of sparkling water as they joined my cheering.

That was better. Leena smiled at me, drawing cards for her turn. She played Paris of Troy, a hero card, to attack her opponent's divine favor points. I didn't know much about the game, but those points were important. Once you lost them, the game was done.

Damon practically growled. "Seriously?"

Apparently he didn't like Leena's team winning. Which meant he had no taste. "Seriously! She's doing great, right?"

"She?" He frowned. "Oh, Kai's teammate. Yeah,

she's all right."

"All right?" I crossed my arms. This guy was an ass. "She's amazing!" I cupped my hands around my mouth. "Great job, Leena! Keep playing those good-looking cards."

I winked at her even though she probably couldn't see it from there. She'd mentioned she could hear me when I sat this close though, so I always tried to get a front-row seat.

"Anyone who teams up with Kai is an idiot," Damon muttered, barely looking at me. "I hope Dionysus' vines tear their cards apart."

Well, if that's how he wanted to play it, then he deserved a wake-up call. He should have sat on the other side of the field if he wanted to cheer for the Drunken Duelists. He definitely shouldn't have called Leena an idiot, no matter how terrible her choice in partners was.

I pulled the water I'd spread out around the crowd back to me, making sure a big splash of it dropped on Damon's head. Served him right. He sputtered, glaring like he wanted to strangle me right here in front of everyone. Maybe antagonizing him had been the wrong move...

"Sorry. It slipped?" I smiled, glancing around to see if another seat was open nearby. Running away after poking the bear was kind of cowardly, but I'd accept it.

He grumbled, pulling his shirt up to wipe off his face and giving me a good view of his toned abs. Whoa. I'd gladly risk that glare of his if it meant getting a peek at those again. Except, the higher he pulled his shirt, the more his beautiful abs turned into horrific scars that looked like claw marks.

"What happened?" I instinctively reached out, my fingers close enough to feel the heat from his body. He'd gone through something terrible. A monster attack, maybe?

He jerked his shirt down. "Nothing."

I dropped my hand, feeling awkward. I shouldn't have asked, not when it was probably a terrible memory. He rearranged his sopping wet hair, covering a pretty bad looking scar around his eye too. Was that why he let his hair grow out so much?

"They're a terrible team, you know. Don't bother cheering for them." He wrung his shirt out, giving me a sideways look like he knew I could pull the water from it easily, but wasn't offering to help. "They make up lies and discredit other duelists just to get ahead."

Asking about his scars had obviously touched a nerve, but that didn't mean he could badmouth Leena.

"I'm not cheering for them. I'm cheering for

her." I nodded at Leena. "She's my friend and I'm here to support her. I'd be cheering even if she was completely losing. It doesn't matter. And she's not the kind of person to make up lies. If anything, that's Kai's doing, so don't blame her."

Bubbles swirled through my body as my water started boiling. Soon it would be impossible to hide how annoyed I was, so it was best to leave before causing a scene. Humans had it so much easier, hiding their emotions whenever they wanted.

I spotted an empty seat a few rows up and grabbed my bag. When I moved, his hand jerked out, grasping my arm to pull me back down.

"Wait. I'm sorry I called your friend an idiot. Don't go." His eyes met mine, pleading with me to stay. It was a look I couldn't resist, not when he was still drenched because of me. He hadn't actually gotten mad about that either, so maybe I'd misjudged him.

I paused, hoping to lighten the mood. "Eager to get doused with more water?"

I expected him to roll his eyes or to mutter something about how annoying I was, but instead, his gaze darted to the cameras flying over the arena. "If that's what it takes. Just stay."

His grip on my arm was light, but I could feel his desperation. I nodded, sitting back down casually as if I'd just been readjusting. Cameras covered the Shimmering Isles, capturing the duelists' lives as much as they could. The TV station wanted every opportunity to get more viewers, even if it meant invading people's lives. Apparently that was part of their contract, so he shouldn't be upset by it now. Which meant something else was going on.

"What's wrong?" I asked.

"If you run away, Kai will tell people it was my fault." He ran a hand over his face, pausing over his scar. "That I scared you away because I'm a monster."

Ah. So he didn't like Kai either. That made him instantly more likable.

"Sounds like him." I shrugged, watching Leena reflect an attack back at the Drunken Duelists with Aphrodite's mirror. "If you let him know he's getting to you, he'll never stop."

Damon sighed. "I just want to duel." His eyes darted to me, as if he still expected me to run away screaming in terror. "It's nice that you cheer for your friend."

My friend. He'd picked up on me not liking him talking bad about her and quickly changed his tune. Sure, he was scary to look at, but so were gorgons and cyclops, and some of them were the nicest people.

I settled into my seat, giving Damon my

wickedest grin. "So what you're saying is, I'm so cool that you wish I'd cheer for you too?"

His mouth dropped open and I couldn't help but laugh. He was fun to tease. Maybe I would go to one of his games. I couldn't picture him standing in front of a crowd and putting on a show. He seemed far too introverted for that, but what did I know? Maybe he was a different person when he dueled.

He crossed his arms, acting like he was focusing on the game again, but he kept frowning at me. Finally he said, "It wouldn't be so bad."

My eyebrows shot up. Did he actually want me to cheer for him? I bit my lip, trying not to laugh and have him think I was making fun of him. If he was open to me cheering for him, maybe he'd be open to the idea of letting me become his hairstylist too. I'd use that scowl of his as inspiration, making him look like the sexy, brooding type of guy that so many fans fell for. I could practically see it now...

"You're doing it again." When I didn't answer, he sighed. "You're staring."

I winced. "Sorry. I just..." I was probably about to cross another line here, but if he really wanted to become a great duelist, he needed lots of fans. "Have you ever considered a different hairstyle?"

"You sound like the TV station, wanting me to

look more appealing for their viewers." His scowl deepened. "As if I look this way by choice."

"Did they really tell you that?"

"They suggested I try looking more like *him*." The glare he shot at Kai could freeze oceans. "Like he wasn't the one who started all this nonsense in the first place. He's been egging the fans on to get me kicked off the island. All because I don't fit his image of a duelist."

I frowned. "Well, he doesn't fit my image of what a duelist should be either. So don't mind him."

Now I wanted to make Damon look dark and brooding even more, to shove it in Kai's face that people with any kind of looks could duel. He didn't have the right to change everyone like he was changing Leena. This could be beneficial for both of us. Damon would get the TV station off his back while I'd get another duelist on my client list. Sticking it to Kai was just the cherry on top.

"You know," I paused, waiting for him to look at me. "I bet I can style your hair in a way that'll piss Kai off and make the TV station happy."

He snorted. "Right. And I bet all the ladies would be swooning over me."

He shook his head, laughing for the first time. It wasn't a cheerful laugh though; it was a self-deprecating one. I wanted to know more about him, this mystery man who sat down next to me. But it was more than curiosity. I wanted to help him flourish on this island and get past whatever had happened to him instead of letting Kai drag him down. I was losing that fight with Leena, but I could help Damon.

"Damn straight you'll have people swooning over you." I held out my hand. "Let's make this bet official. If I win, you agree to become an official, lifelong client of mine."

He eyed my hand like it might bite him. "And if this all goes horribly wrong and I win?"

"Then I'll come cheer for you at your next duel." I grinned, reaching my hand closer to him. "I'll even be extra ridiculous, making sure the whole crowd's into it."

"Like I'd want that." He scoffed, but his smile looked genuine this time. He did want that, which meant I'd cheer for him win or lose. How could I not support an underdog like him? But I needed him to agree to the bet first. He sighed, finally taking my hand. "Fine. But you better not make me look like some pretty boy."

I laughed. "I'll avoid frosted tips and highlights."

His eyes widened like he hadn't even considered those options. "Great..."

"Meet me tomorrow at 6:00 p.m. I promise

you won't regret it." I handed him a business card for the salon where I worked.

He took it carefully, like it was precious to him. The more time I spent with Damon, the more curious I became. Why was such a sweet guy hiding himself behind an angry exterior? A few scars didn't make him a monster.

Before I could tell him that, a cheer rose around us, signaling the end of the match. I glanced at the floating lanterns. Leena had won. I should probably go congratulate her right away, but part of me wanted to keep this conversation going.

"I'll see you tomorrow?" I stood up, but didn't leave until he nodded in agreement.

He called out as I walked away. "My next duel isn't for a week, so you've got time to prepare."

"Yeah, right. I'm winning this bet, Damon!" I laughed, waving at him.

He had no idea what was in store for him. He seemed like he needed a win and I was going to get it for him. I planned on making him so darkly sexy that the fans would beg to see him, leaving the TV station no choice but to accept him. And I'd be one step closer to becoming an actual hairstylist instead of being stuck doing blowouts. It was a win for both of us.

CHAPTER 2 – DAMON

The closer I got to the hair salon, the slower my feet moved. My brother, Leo, stifled a yawn, lazily matching his wheelchair to my slower pace. Six in the evening was pretty early by Shimmering Isles standards, but Chantara had picked the time. It wasn't like me being wide awake would help this situation at all anyway.

She'd seemed confident she could get the TV station to approve of me, but if she was wrong, my brother and I were in trouble. Since the entire island revolved around dueling, there was no place for a team that wasn't pulling in enough viewers for the TV station to make money. Which meant they could kick us off the island if the fans kept thinking I was terrifying.

"What's wrong?" The metal wings on the back of my brother's wheelchair stopped beating, folding into the back as he looked at me. "Regretting this bet of yours?"

"You know I am." I rubbed my hand over my face, trying to avoid staring at the empty air where his leg should have been.

It was the whole reason we were here: to win enough money for the Atlantean blacksmiths to forge him a new leg. But I was holding him back. I hadn't even defended him properly in our last duel and a fire blast hit him, burning his arm. Maybe he should find a different teammate...

"It'll be fine." He pulled his long blond hair into a ponytail that many people fawned over. He was either a lot stronger than me mentally or those good looks of his had helped him stay confident even after what we'd gone through. "I'll charm this water nymph you met, get her to convince her friend that we deserve to duel Kai, and we'll show off your new awesome haircut. The fans will love us, the TV station will beg us for more screen time, and we'll be filthy rich in no time."

He sounded so sure of himself, like he had

no doubt that all those things would happen. His plans did tend to work out, but this one relied on me looking less scary and on Chantara being able to talk Kai into dueling us. Neither of which sounded likely.

We had to keep trying though. Beating a fan favorite like Kai would really shake things up and put him in his place for once, but he'd been adamantly refusing our requests to duel him. He didn't think I was worth his time. Which was why the TV station wanting me to be more like him cut so deep. I'd never willingly be like that jerk.

I started walking toward the salon again. "What if Chantara's not so easily charmed?"

"I'll just work extra hard then." My brother winked at me, catching up with one strong beat of his wheelchair's wings. "So, on a scale of harpy to goddess, how hot is this mystical water nymph?"

He said it casually, but I could tell he was curious. Which kind of irritated me. Chantara wasn't just a means to get what we wanted. She was more than that. She was a nice person and didn't deserve my playboy brother giving her ideas he wouldn't follow through on.

"Look, why don't I just handle this myself?"

My brother snorted. "I'd pay to see you flirting with somebody."

My face burned as I remembered the bet included me making random strangers swoon. Why had I agreed to such an embarrassing bet? There was no way my brother could stay and watch that. I had to get rid of him somehow.

"Are you... blushing?" He leaned forward to get a better look. "You are! You actually want to flirt with her, don't you?"

"Don't be ridiculous." I stormed off toward the salon again, feeling the whoosh of air stirred by his wheelchair's wings as he followed.

Flirting with Chantara was something I might have tried once, before the chimera attack left me looking like a mangled ragdoll. We really needed that duel with Kai, so I should've gone with Leo's plan, but I really didn't want to watch her fall for his charm. For her sake, of course, not because I wished she would fall for me or anything. Ugh. This whole thing was going to be a disaster.

My brother zoomed ahead of me, peeking inside the salon's windows before I caught up with him. He turned around, his eyebrows high.

"So she's goddess level and you're trying to keep her to yourself. I see how it is." He crossed his arms, spinning his chair to pin me with an accusatory look. "Sure you're only here for the bet?"

I rolled my eyes. "What else would I be here for?"

"Love, desire, flirting." He sighed. "Human interaction. Don't you miss that?"

"No." I glanced down at his arm covered in fading healing runes from our last duel. If I'd realized how dangerous the live version of this game was, I'd have found a different way to raise the money.

My brother was determined to duel though, remembering how much we'd loved it before the attack. Coming here had always been our dream and he wasn't willing to give it up, no matter how damaged his body got. It wasn't right.

As if he could read my thoughts, my brother sighed again, heavier this time. "You can't keep holding onto the past forever, Damon. We're both alive and living out our dream." He patted my arm. "It's time to move on."

Move on. Like it was that easy. He wasn't the one who'd wanted to go exploring that day. He wasn't the one drowning in guilt. The bell above the shop door rang, pulling me out of my depressing thoughts before they got too bad this time.

"Coming inside?" Chantara leaned out, smiling at us. "Or are you chickening out?"

"Not a chance." My brother pushed me forward with extra oomph from his wheelchair. "He's excited."

I swatted him away. "Let's just get this over with."

"This is you excited?" Chantara held the door open for us, bending down to whisper something to my brother that made him laugh.

I raised an eyebrow at him, but he just shrugged with a secretive grin as he whispered back to Chantara. They were either laughing at my expense or he was flirting with her, neither of which sounded good.

"Don't you have a healing appointment today?" I stepped in front of the door before he came inside.

"It can wait." His grin widened. "Unless you don't want me to see you making women swoon?"

I glared at Chantara. "You told him what the bet was?"

She held her hands up innocently. "I didn't know it was a secret."

Except she told him the first opportunity she had. Which meant she probably assumed I hadn't told anyone. It was just so embarrassing. I didn't want to picture the end of this when I'd have to make women swoon. How did somebody even do that on the spot? And what exactly counted as swooning?

"I'll leave you two to it then." My brother winked at me, then turned toward the healing district, flinging open his wheelchair's wings. After he gained a bit of momentum, the chair lifted into the air, reminding me that I was the only thing keeping him on the ground. He turned around to yell one last thing. "I expect pictures!"

"Oh, there will be tons." Chantara's eyes lit up. She was enjoying this far too much.

She led me to an empty chair, motioning for me to sit down. The shop was unnaturally quiet, with three empty chairs next to me. I frowned at the empty hair-washing stations, which were usually packed with duelists getting ready for their duels. I'd quickly learned the word blowout when I moved here, but I'd never had a reason to get one myself. Pretty hair wouldn't fix my scars.

"Where is everyone?" My voice sounded too loud in the silent salon. I really wished we hadn't made this bet. What was I doing here?

"We're not quite open yet." Chantara shrugged, as if she'd made a silly mistake even though she was the one who'd set the time.

I knew 6:00 p.m. felt too early to be here. Since everyone who lived on the Shimmering Isles was here to support the duelists, and duels only happened at night, the place was basically nocturnal. Had she intentionally invited me here early so I wouldn't scare off her other customers?

I shifted awkwardly in my seat while she arranged a bowl of water and various scissors and combs around the counter. She turned my chair to face the mirror and stood behind me, studying my hair. Then she summoned a ball of water as if from thin air, the blob hovering over my head just like at the duel.

"You're not going to try drowning me again, are you?" I leaned away, not sure what I'd done to annoy her this time.

She rolled her eyes. "Drown you? That's a bit dramatic." She swirled the water through my hair, washing it without wasting a single drop. "You'd be dead if I tried to drown you."

Was she serious or joking? I dared a quick glance at her, meeting her ocean-blue eyes in the mirror. The corner of her mouth quirked up in a smile as she guided the water through my hair and into a nearby sink. My muddy brown hair practically shimmered in the bright lights of the salon. I bet she had a ton of clients if just washing their hair with her magical water made this much of an improvement.

My hair was fully dry already too, as if she'd pulled every bit of water from it. Which meant she'd left me sopping wet yesterday on purpose.

"Oh, don't look at me like that." She scoffed. "No wonder you scare everyone away."

I dropped my gaze, snapping back to reality. "Sorry."

How was I supposed to convince her to ask her

friend for a favor if I couldn't even have a normal conversation without scaring her? If only this bet of hers succeeded. If she could get people to like me, then I wouldn't have to worry about getting kicked off the island anymore. My brother and I could just duel and we'd eventually win everything we needed. That sounded like the kind of wishful thinking Leo spouted though. I knew better.

"No, I'm the one who's sorry." Chantara kneeled, looking me in the eyes. "I am not afraid of you."

The silence stretched as she held my gaze for longer than anyone ever had. Long enough for it to get super awkward. Was she waiting for me to say I believed her, or what?

She reached forward, holding my hair at different lengths and angles, mumbling to herself. Her intense focus made me want to curl up and hide. When was the last time anyone had looked at me with such genuine interest? I knew she was just excited to cut my hair, but the butterflies in my stomach hoped for more.

After what felt like hours, she grinned wickedly. "You trust me, right?"

I'd seen similar grins on my brother too many times to not know when somebody had a crazy idea. I had no clue what her idea might be, but she seemed to have fun messing with me, so it was probably a terrible one. She was easy to read too; that spark in her eyes was full of mischief.

"I just met you..."

"Then you have no reason not to trust me." She put her hand on my shoulder, squeezing it briefly as she stood back up. "I'm going to give you a hairstyle that'll let you be yourself, but have everyone falling for you."

That sounded a bit too perfect to be true, but maybe, just maybe, she'd pull it off. Most hairstylists tried to make me look as different as possible, like somebody attractive and approachable. It once ended with a child crying when I smiled at them. Chantara's attempts probably wouldn't be any different, but I couldn't squash the ray of hope her smile gave me. Plus, I had agreed to the bet, so I couldn't back out now.

I straightened in the chair, readying myself. "It can't really get any worse, so just do it."

"Mind if I use that as a review?" She laughed. "It can't get any worse, so just do it?"

I rolled my eyes, trying not to flinch as she cut huge chunks of my hair off on one side. With just a few snips, she exposed my facial scars completely. I clutched the chair's plastic arms, panic coursing through me.

"What are you doing?" My voice came out

higher than I'd meant it to.

She froze. "Cutting your hair?"

The scars that had changed my life mocked me in the mirror. They were all I could see, those angry lines where the beast's claws had shredded me like paper. Chantara had gotten rid of the parts of my hair I hid behind. Every other hairstylist tried to cover up my scars as much as possible, so I hadn't thought to mention it to her. This wouldn't end well.

"Sorry. I can't do this." I got up, shaking my head as I fumbled to get around her, but she stood firmly in my way.

"You can't leave now, not when I've only just started. What will people think?" She put her hands on my shoulders, guiding me back to the seat. "It will look great. Just give me a chance to show you."

"How can it with this?" I motioned at my scar. Hiding it had always been my best option. Now I'd have to get a hat or something.

"You should never have to hide." She leaned down, meeting my eyes in the mirror. "Your scars show everyone that you've survived something awful. That you are strong. Fearless."

She picked up her scissors again and paused, as if waiting for my approval. She was right. I couldn't be a coward and leave in the middle of this. I looked even scarier than usual at the moment.

"If you say so." I nodded, letting her continue.

Nobody had ever said I looked fearless before. When I looked in the mirror, all I saw was that scared boy who wouldn't leave the house for a year because people kept staring at him. Coming to this island with all the cameras had been a nightmare, but it got better when I realized nobody wanted to look at me. Their eyes kind of just glossed over me and focused on my brother instead.

"So..." Chantara's voice trailed off a bit, but her hands kept moving confidently through my hair. "Do you mind telling me what happened to you and your brother?" Her scissors stopped for a moment. "You don't have to if you're not comfortable. I just hate believing rumors online and would rather get the truth from the source."

"You're the only one." I took a deep breath, steadying myself as she started cutting again. The snipping sounds were oddly soothing. "I used to love exploring as a teenager. My brother and I would go anywhere, brave any environment, if it meant finding something cool."

Chantara nodded as she grabbed a hair clipper to buzz one side of my head. The side with my scar, of course. Why was she making that a focal point by leaving the other side nice and long? There was no way I could step outside looking like this. My stomach clenched as I looked away.

I must have been frowning, because she tapped her finger between my eyebrows, right next to my scars. "You'll get wrinkles."

"Wrinkles? I've got all these scars, but you're worried about wrinkles?" I laughed, laughed so hard she had to stop working because I was bent nearly in half.

Eventually my laughter caught on and she joined in. For the first time in years, somebody didn't care about my scars or how scary I looked. She was acting like I was just a client getting their hair cut, not a monster. My muscles loosened as I leaned back in the chair, calming down.

"Ready to continue?" she asked, barely even waiting for my nod.

Sitting here, listening to her hum a song I didn't recognize, put me at ease more than any therapist ever had. I could finish telling her my story.

"Three years ago, we were exploring farther away than usual, but just couldn't seem to find anything interesting. We'd seen it all before and I was..." bored. That was why my brother had lost a leg that day. Because I'd been too bored with our surroundings to stop searching when he asked me to. To go back home, where it was safe. I'd give anything to have stayed home that day.

Chantara put down her scissors. Her eyes were pinched in sadness, like she knew how this story was going to end. I wasn't ready to hear what she had to say though, worried she'd pity me, or worse, blame me.

"Anyway." I cleared my throat. "It was hot out that day, so we were going to take a break under a nice big tree for shade. Apparently, chimeras also like big, shady areas."

I shrugged, acting like it was no big deal. That's how my brother always told the story. With lots of excitement and funny moments, like it hadn't been the worst day of our lives. We'd barely gotten away. If it hadn't been for a group of adventurers hunting the creature, we wouldn't have survived.

"And, well, you know the rest." I forced a laugh, feeling the guilt start to overwhelm me. I was the only reason my brother was there that day. He'd rescheduled a date just to hang out with me, his poor, bored brother. And I'd... I'd almost gotten him killed.

The smell of ammonia pulled me from my thoughts. Chantara was casually mixing up hair dye as if I wasn't an emotional wreck. She really was a nice person. I took a few deep breaths. In and out. In and out. When I was calm enough, she came back over, smiling at me.

"What do you think about a darker hair color?" Her eyes were twinkling again. She was up to something.

Darker hair would make me look scarier, but I already looked pretty horrific, so why not?

"Sure." My lips pressed into a thin line that hopefully resembled a smile. "I trust you."

She grinned, slapping the hair dye on quickly, like she was worried I'd change my mind. Or like she was a mad scientist doing an experiment on me. I shivered as the cold dye coated my hair.

The bell above the door rang as a few women walked in, talking and laughing with each other.

"Hey, Chantara."

They greeted her with familiarity, so I assumed they worked here. The noises of a busy shop filled the air as they all gathered their equipment and readied their stations. I hunched over in my seat, trying to angle myself so they wouldn't see my scars. Getting a hat really would be my first priority when I got out of here. Maybe I should text my brother to get one. No. Then he'd ask me how this was going and I couldn't tell him it was a massive fail. Not yet.

"This dye is going to get all over you if you don't sit up straight," Chantara chided.

I forced myself to sit up, my back ramrod

straight and my eyes squeezed shut. This was all just too much. Why had I ever agreed to this bet? That thought would haunt me for the months it took to grow my hair out again.

As I sat there, waiting for the dye to do its magic, other clients streamed in, chatting happily with each other. It sounded like most of them were just there to get their hair washed and styled before their duels. Chantara would probably need to go help them soon, except she just kept quietly cleaning her station. I was pretty sure she'd swept the floor four times already. She probably felt bad leaving me here. I guess I was pretty pathetic with my eyes closed.

I opened them, blinking in the bright salon lights. "You can go help them if you need to."

"Not a chance." She shook her head, setting the broom aside. "It's time to wash that dye out. Can't wait for the big reveal!"

She turned my chair away from the mirror like she didn't want to spoil the fun by letting me see what she was doing. I was fine with whatever made her happy. It wasn't like I really wanted to see this new hairstyle anyway.

She pulled water to her from the bowl on the counter instead of summoning it like before, rinsing my hair until there wasn't any dye left. When my hair felt dry again, she leaned toward me, her hands on the arms of my chair.

"Are you ready?" Her voice was alluring, making me wish I could say yes and mean it. But I was far too nervous. What if it looked horrible? What if the TV station kicked me off the island on sight?

She spun me around. My hair was so dark the shadows devoured any light that touched it. The long side swept over my eye in what might have looked wispy and cool on somebody else, but on me, it just emphasized my shockingly red eyes, terrifying anyone who dared to meet my gaze. The shaved side showed off my scars for the world to see as if I was trying to keep everyone at a distance. I looked... utterly terrifying. My shoulders drooped as the tiny bit of hope I had disappeared.

"What do you think?" Her voice was full of anticipation. "I know you said people tried to brighten you up before, but I figured why not lean in to your dark and brooding qualities."

Lean into my dark side? She was really misjudging the situation, but I didn't have the heart to tell her that, not when she was so excited.

"It's great." The lie sounded hollow, but it was the best I could do. I didn't think I could look more frightening, but she'd managed it.

"You hate it, don't you?" She leaned against a table, looking way sadder than I expected her to. I should be the sad one here, not her.

"No." I jumped up, wanting to comfort her, but having no clue how to do it. "It's just really different, that's all."

She studied me like she was waiting for the awful truth to come out. Then she pulled her phone out and snapped a picture.

"What was that for?" I flinched, not wanting physical evidence of this. I'd have to find another stylist immediately to tone this hairstyle down.

"I promised your brother." She winked at me, then turned to everyone else that I suddenly remembered were here. They were staring at me. All of them. Where was Hades' invisibility helm when you needed it? "What do you guys think?"

One of the other stylists walked over, nodding appreciatively. "That I should have let you style people's hair months ago."

"Wait." My eyes widened. "You're not actually a hairstylist?"

"Well, I mostly do blowouts since I've got magical water skills and everything." Chantara shrugged in that innocent of course I didn't trick you on purpose way of hers. "But I've styled Leena's hair many times!"

Ugh. I'd never make a bet with a stranger again. With this terrifying new look, nobody would ever want to duel me. My brother and I would never get a duel with Kai, let alone get to stay here. His dream was going to die with a haircut. He was going to be in a wheelchair for the rest of his life.

"You think they hate it, don't you?" Chantara motioned to the other clients and her coworkers. "But those are the adoring looks of people who think you're hot and I'm awesome."

Yeah, right. Nobody here thought that, otherwise they wouldn't be whispering to each other and giving me those shocked looks. Looks that clearly said whoa, look at that terrifying guy! What does Chantara think she's doing? Or something like that. I'd heard many variations of it.

"I've got to go." I tried to bolt past her, but once again, she stood in my way. She was being entirely ridiculous now. "Look, I'm sorry this didn't work out, but you don't have to lie to me."

"Lie to you?" Chantara frowned. "You really don't believe me, do you?"

Of course I didn't. How could I?

She crossed her arms, standing squarely like she was ready to challenge me to a duel right here and now. "Finish the bet."

"The bet?" My eyes widened. "You can't possibly expect me to, well to..."

I gestured to the other women in the room,

knowing full well Chantara knew what I was talking about. I was not going to try to make them swoon. Not now, when I knew they were even more terrified of me than before. This bet had already been decided. Chantara lost.

Chantara looked like she was waiting for me to finish my sentence, but then deflated a bit when she realized I wasn't going to.

"Fine." She linked her arm through mine, pulling me toward the salon's waiting area where it was quieter. "If you can't bring yourself to try to flirt—"

I snorted, but she continued before I could say anything else.

"Then we should double down." Her voice was calm, sweet even. She was probably going to suggest something even less fun than this haircut. "This new look of yours needs a new wardrobe to go with it."

"You want me to go shopping?" I glanced at her sideways to see if she was kidding, but I honestly couldn't tell. Her default setting seemed to be mischief. "Why?"

"First, to give you time to realize how good you look." Her gaze raked me up and down. "Because I did a damn good job here."

"And second?" I forced through clenched teeth.

"I want your brother as a client too." She glanced at the stylist who I assumed was her boss. "If I can get a few more duelist clients, I'll be able to make a name for myself finally. You can help me do that and I'll help you win the TV station over."

"So you want to use me?"

The entrance was just a few steps away. I should get out of here before I agreed to another bet with her that would end terribly. But I liked the feel of her arm linked through mine, of her standing close enough to me to whisper.

"I want to help you. Help us both, actually." She moved in front of me, looking me straight in the eyes. "I bet I can make the TV station put you in a prime-time duel by the end of the week. If I win, both you and your brother will be my clients."

"That will never happen." I shook my head, smiling at her intense optimism. It was like she didn't think she could ever lose. I could use that. "Fine, but when you fail, you have to convince Kai to duel us."

There. I did it. My brother would be proud. I held my hand out to her, wanting to make the bet official, but she didn't move.

"What's wrong? You were the one who wanted the bet."

She winced. "I know, but Kai is horrible. Convincing him to do anything always comes with a price."

"Then I guess you better not lose." Whether she won or lost this bet, it would work out for me, making up for this terrible haircut she'd given me.

"I won't lose." She gripped my hand tight, sealing the deal. "Meet me in the shopping district by Rhapso's Stitch at 3:00 a.m. after my shift."

I nodded, grateful I'd gotten out of this without trying to make anyone swoon. Small victory, but I could only handle so much in one day. I needed to get home and prepare for what would probably be an exhausting shopping trip.

"See you soon." Chantara waved goodbye, smiling like she really was excited to be around me.

My stomach flip-flopped. I could get used to her looking at me like that...

I managed a nod before fleeing the salon, my face burning. Nobody would ever fall for somebody who looked like me. Getting close to her was setting myself up for pain, but it was a risk I had to take. For my brother and our dueling career, but mainly for myself. I wanted to bask in the glow of her happiness for as long as I could.

CHAPTER 3 – CHANTARA

Leena and I stood outside Rhapso's Stitch, half an hour past my meeting time with Damon.

"He's not going to show." Leena ran her fingers through her newly dyed blond hair, a frown on her face as if she disliked the new style.

That's why I hadn't wanted to do it, but she'd insisted, saying Kai had done a lot of research and pretty blond duelists were what the fans wanted right now. If she kept following his ideas, she wouldn't even recognize herself in a few months. She kept telling me it was what she wanted, though, that all these changes would help her gain fans.

I just didn't see it. I'd liked who she was when I first met her, a woman full of fire and passion for the game. Not this person who second-guessed everything based on whether the fans would like it or not.

I sighed, not wanting to get into that argument again today. "He'll show."

The look on his face when he'd seen what I'd done to his hair had been heartbreaking. All I wanted to do was help him shine, but I could tell he hated it. He wore his emotions on his sleeve, so obvious to anyone paying attention. If he'd just let the fans in instead of shying away from them, they'd all see what a softie he was on the inside. And everyone loved a dark and sexy exterior concealing a heart of gold.

I really believed I could get the TV station to stop trying to kick him off the island, but only if he showed up today. Maybe I'd freaked him out too much. Maybe he thought I had no idea what I was talking about. Maybe...

Damon shuffled into the shopping district, barely recognizable with a beanie pulled low over his eyes, covering the beautiful hairstyle I'd given him as much as possible.

I raised an eyebrow. "You hated it that much, huh?"

"No." He blushed, reaching for the hat as if he wanted to verify it was still in place. "I just didn't want people to see it until I had the full style you promised."

I rolled my eyes as Leena's eyebrows flew up in disbelief.

How could I help Damon see what I saw in him? I could already tell he wouldn't believe the truth, that I'd found him incredibly attractive even before the haircut. That I'd gotten lost staring into his eyes when I was supposed to be checking if my cuts were straight. Or that afterward, I'd stared at the picture I'd taken of him for far longer than I'd like to admit.

"Sorry I'm late," he mumbled, his face pinched in pain. It was like being out in public physically hurt him somehow. "I was..."

His fingers readjusted the hat again, making me think he was late because he was too self-conscious. Maybe I shouldn't have been so bold with his haircut. My heart ached for him. He'd survived a chimera attack. He should be proud of himself, not ashamed of his scars. Without thinking about it, I reached out and grabbed his hand. His eyes widened, but before he could pull away, I tightened my grip.

"I'll forgive you." My lips pulled into a sly smile. "If

you try on whatever I suggest, no questions asked."

"Oh boy," Leena said ominously. "That sounds scary even to me."

Damon glanced between me and the door to the clothing store, his hand only loosely holding mine. An internal debate flashed across his eyes. This was probably too much for him. I should back off.

"You don't—"

"Deal." Damon flung the door open wide, striding into the clothing store like he was marching to his death, unwilling to show fear anymore. His fingers laced through mine, clutching my hand like he had no intention of letting me go.

His new confident, take-charge attitude sent a shiver of desire through me as he pulled me into the store behind him. His muscular back was strong, like he'd been chiseled from marble. The weapons he wore that had scared me at first now made me wonder how good he was at using them. Did he practice every day? A montage of him shirtless and sweating as he sparred ran through my mind. I wouldn't mind seeing that.

Leena leaned in close to whisper. "You forgot to mention you're completely into him."

"What?" I laughed, casually trying to let go of his hand, but he had a vise grip on me like he needed the extra support.

I wasn't into him; I was just trying to comfort him. When I liked somebody, I put everything I had into the relationship. I didn't half-ass anything important to me, which was why I'd sworn off guys until I got promoted. No distractions for me. No matter how dark and adorable they were...

Damon didn't stop to look at any clothes; he just strode straight ahead like he didn't know what else to do now that he'd charged in here. Which was fine by me. I'd already called ahead and asked Rhapso to pull some clothes off the racks for us. Damon was walking straight toward a collection of outfits meant to seduce his fans into giving in to their dark desires. I'd purposefully requested villainous outfits, sinfully sexy ones that would change Damon's entire persona. Because if the TV station wanted a good show, I'd give them one. Everyone loved a good villain.

"Welcome to my store." Rhapso let go of the outfit she was working on, which floated into the air while the needles kept sewing it. Multiple outfits swooped across the ceiling, needles and thread curling through the air. "You're here for the villain outfits, right?"

"Villain outfits?" Damon practically squeaked, finally stopping his trudge through the store to stare at me. "You planned this?"

I grinned. "Heck yeah, I did. I can't wait to see how good you look trying them on!"

He groaned as Rhapso fluttered about, putting the first outfit behind a magic mirror that would show Damon wearing the costume in its reflection. If he'd step in front of it, that was.

"I know I said no questions asked," I paused, afraid I was pushing him too far. "But I don't want you to be miserable either."

He was silent as he studied the rack of black dueling costumes Rhapso had picked out for us, pops of color drawing the eye here and there. I looked at Leena, nodding for her to jump in any time now. That was the whole reason I brought her: to give a duelist's perspective, not to shop for herself.

She pulled away from a slinky pink Aphrodite outfit and browsed through the villain ones. "These will definitely get the fans' attention."

Rhapso's smile widened. "I thought so too! The moment Chantara said who they were for, I knew exactly what to pick."

Damon frowned. "Why do you all want me to be even scarier? That's why fans don't like me, remember?"

I was messing this all up. He still thought he was a monster and here I was trying to force evil-looking clothes on him. He probably thought I was afraid of him too. I had to nip this in the bud before it got worse, otherwise I'd never be able to help him.

"Just trust me." I put my hand on his back, nudging him toward the mirror. "There's a difference between looking scary and actually being scary." I kept my voice low, as if saying this quietly might stop him from running away from me again. "The first can be pretty hot, but the second is what people are actually worried about and that's definitely not you."

He was looking at the ground instead of the mirror, so he didn't see the gorgeous way the black coat he wore clung to his muscles, sweeping wide behind him like shadows. He didn't see how the opening drew my eyes to his abs, how the sparkling chains swooping from one side of the coat to the other enhanced the look of the daggers in his belt. He didn't see how his red eyes popped, the only bit of color making sure people paid attention to them. He didn't see any of it because he was unwilling to look.

"Damon?"

Rhapso and Leena walked away, looking at the Aphrodite outfit for Leena, giving us some space. They could probably sense this wasn't quite going as planned.

I moved in between Damon and the mirror.

"We don't have to do this if you don't want to."

His eyes squeezed shut as he took a deep breath, then he finally looked me in the eye. "You really think this will work?"

"I really do." I reached out for his hat, but paused before my fingers actually touched it. "You are beautiful, inside and out. These scars that you're trying to hide are part of who you are. They show how brave you are. How strong you are. If you let your fans in, let them see the real you, they'll never be scared of you again. They'll see you exactly how I see you."

"And how's that?" For once he didn't look away, but his face was full of confusion. He really had no idea.

"That you're sweet, but too afraid of what others think to show it. That you protect the people you care about no matter the cost to yourself. That you're kind and bashful and adorable and all the things I—"

Love about a guy. Wow, I was getting in way over my head here. This was a business trip, not a date. I cleared my throat, smiling at my ridiculousness. "And all the things fans will really love. If you show them instead of keeping quiet and avoiding everyone."

He ripped his hat off, stuffing it into his pocket as a blush burned across his face. He stepped around me to finally look in the mirror and crossed his arms, staring at his reflection like he wanted to pummel it. Maybe that hadn't been the right outfit choice after all.

"I think it looks great, but we could try something else."

Rhapso casually reappeared, as if she'd been waiting for us to need her again. "I've got all sorts of ideas for you. If you don't want to show that much skin, we can try—"

"No." Damon shook his head. "If Chantara likes it, then this one is fine."

"What I like doesn't matter." I motioned at the rack of other options. "I'm sure there's something in here you'll like too."

He smiled, just a tiny smile, but it was there. "I like this one."

It sure hadn't seemed like he did a moment ago, but who was I to second-guess him? He probably didn't want to be in this store anymore, subjected to whatever other outfits Rhapso picked for him. Between this and the haircut, he was probably overwhelmed.

"Ok, well, what about different weapons then?" He seemed to like those, so maybe that would give him something fun to look at. "Rhapso found a few jeweled daggers that will draw people's attention."

Rhapso brought out an assortment of costume swords and daggers that would fit his look. Since Leena was an Aphrodite duelist, we rarely ended up in the weapons section, but some of these looked impressive. I glanced at Damon to see what he thought, but he was clutching the nondescript daggers at his side like he was terrified. Like the idea of giving those up was too much.

"Actually," I shook my head at Rhapso. "I think the ones he has are great."

He sighed, his fingers unclenching. The Shimmering Isles only had fake monsters, but I had a feeling that didn't matter to him. Not after seeing a chimera face-to-face. How could I have asked him to trade his daggers out like they were unimportant?

"We can check out and get going then if you want."

He nodded, but before he could grab the clothes from behind the mirror, a male satyr took a picture of him. He jerked around, his body tense, ready for a fight. This was going downhill fast.

"What do you think you're doing?" I snapped at the duelist. "That's pretty rude, you know."

He held his hands up, eyes wide, like he hadn't expected to get caught. "Sorry. He just looks so good. Who did his makeover?"

Leena sauntered over, beaming. "That's a Chantara original right there. She did his hair and picked out a theme for his costume. Then Rhapso found the perfect outfit."

"Chantara?" The guy looked confused, obviously not realizing that was me. "Could she do mine too?"

"I don't know, can you?" Leena asked me, smiling like this was her plan all along. To get me more customers.

I didn't have time for that, though, no matter how much I wanted to get more business. Damon looked tense, his eyes darting from the rude duelist to a few other people coming near us.

"Sure, stop by the shop, and I'll see what I can do." I snagged the clothes from behind the mirror and handed them to Rhapso. "But we're running late. Sorry!"

The satyr nodded. "No problem. Do you have a business card?"

I scrounged for the last one I had, handing it to him. I'd given my only other card out to Damon the first day we'd met. The idea of having to print more was exciting. If only Damon didn't look so uncomfortable right now.

Damon sighed as the duelist walked away, putting his hat back on. Whatever moment we'd had was gone and he was back to hating how he looked. Even after that duelist had loved the new look. What would it take to break him of his misbelief about himself? To really get him to love himself again? Maybe I should ask his brother about it. Or maybe that was totally crossing a line. I was just his hairstylist after all. What gave me the right to butt into his life like that?

Leena shook her head at me. "That was the perfect opportunity to get your name out there."

"Sometimes there are more important things than fame." Like making sure Damon didn't have a panic attack because of me.

"And that's why you're still a blowout girl." Leena winced, like she just realized how cruel that had sounded. It wasn't my fault my magical water made me the best suited for washing hair. "Sorry. What I meant was you could open your own salon with how talented you are. You just need to get your name out there and focus on yourself more."

Instead of helping everyone else was what her look implied. It was hard to see people struggling and not help, but she was right. I'd already wasted too many years helping my family and friends back home when I should have been letting them stand on their own two feet. At some point, me helping them had become a crutch, one that made it impossible for any of us to live up to our full potential. That's why I'd moved here.

Was helping underdogs like Damon and Leena the same thing, though? No. They were helping me too, or at least that was the idea. I shrugged off my negative thoughts and smiled at Leena.

"Open my own salon?" I laughed. "Be serious. I'm not even officially a hairstylist yet."

Damon joined us again, a lot calmer than before. He ran a hand over his hat. "I bet a shop run by you would do great."

Opening my own salon was a dream I'd had since I was a kid, but it didn't seem practical right now. It would take years, many years, to get the fame and loyal client base I'd need to open my own business. Otherwise, it'd flop in the first few months and then what would I do?

"You really want to bet that?" I winked at him, trying to lighten the mood, but he just nodded at me, completely serious. "But you hate the haircut I gave you."

He mumbled something, then cleared his throat. "It was really... comfortable in your chair. Other people would like it too."

So he liked how comfortable the chair was? No, by the way he was blushing, he liked how comfortable I made him feel while he was there. I smiled. Who would have guessed he felt that way? It was always my goal to make my clients feel safe while they were with me, but he'd reacted so badly to the haircut that I thought I'd screwed up.

But apparently I'd done something right. Something that made him think I could open my own salon even. Somehow, coming from him, it sounded special. Leena rolled her eyes at me like she could tell what I was thinking. We left the shop together, but then Damon paused, as if he wasn't sure what to do now.

"I'll see you again?" he asked.

Right. Now that our two styling appointments were done, I didn't have a reason to see him until his next haircut. Except, our bet wasn't done yet. I'd promised to get the TV station off his back, so I had to deliver. How could I do it?

"Didn't you want to go to the fan event tomorrow?" Leena prompted me, as if we'd had this conversation at some point. Which we hadn't. "You know, the one where any fan can play against their favorite duelist?"

I grinned. "Right, of course. That's the perfect place to showcase your new look." I glanced at Damon, who thankfully wasn't panicking yet. "Are you going?"

"I don't think any fans will show up for me." He shrugged, as if it didn't bother him, but I knew it did. "But Leo really wants to go, so I'll be there."

His eyes turned to me, hopeful. As if he wanted me there too. With him looking at me like that, how could I not show up? Those damn eyes of his were going to get me in trouble one day.

"Then I'll see you tomorrow." I smiled, excitement already coursing through me. Tomorrow could change everything for him. And for me.

CHAPTER 4 – DAMON

Everyone was staring at me even more than usual now that I was wearing this ridiculous outfit Chantara had picked out. She must have used some kind of magic to get me to agree to it, to insist on it even when she'd given me other options. I clutched the edges of the coat together, wishing the fabric didn't show off all the scars on my chest.

Cameras circled the arena, following all the duelists making our way inside for the fan event Leo had convinced me to attend. Between his excitement and the thought of seeing Chantara again, it really hadn't taken that much convincing.

Tables filled the dueling field, offering places for fans to challenge their favorite duelist one-on-one. I should have brought a book in case nobody showed up to duel me. I tried to smile as we looked for our tables, but it must have looked a bit shaky because Leo patted me on the back.

"You look fine, if that's what you're worried about." Leo failed to keep the grin off his face that had been threatening to take over ever since I'd gotten dressed. "I'd even go as far as to say dashing. Intriguing? Sexy?" He laughed, his grin reaching from ear to ear. "Life has been so much fun since you met Chantara."

I groaned as he wheeled himself to the table with his name on it, which thankfully only had one chair by it instead of two so we didn't have to rearrange anything. I'd only met Chantara a few days ago, but she'd already turned my life upside down. From my hair to my clothes, it was like I was a different person. One I wasn't sure I liked yet.

Today was supposed to prove that everything she'd done would get the TV station off my back for good. I really doubted that would happen, but she seemed so convinced it would. I had to at least give it a shot by coming to this event decked out in all my villainous attire. The worst thing that could happen was I'd be a little embarrassed. I'd dealt with that before. I could do it again on the off chance she was right. And if she wasn't, at least I could say I'd tried.

I sat down at the table next to Leo's, glancing at the one next to me to see who'd witness my lack of opponents. My eyes widened as I read the sign.

"You won't believe who's sitting next to us." I nudged Leo, nodding at the neighboring table.

Kai. The asshole who thought I didn't belong here. I had no idea why he was so popular, but beating that pretty-boy would ensure Leo and I got to stay here even if Chantara's well-intentioned plan failed. The fates had smiled on us with this table arrangement.

"He's actually participating this time?" Leo raised his eyebrows. "I thought he'd be worried some talented fan would humiliate him."

That was always a risk, so vain duelists usually avoided these events. You never knew how good a fan would be at the game. Especially when they'd been studying our decks, probably memorizing our every move, while we had no idea what kinds of plays they'd make. It was a setup to make the fans have fun and feel good, which was fine by me. I wouldn't mind being beaten as long as somebody showed up to duel me.

Please, somebody show up to duel me.

Kai strolled in, staring at me like I was a bug he wanted to squash. "We should ask to change locations."

"Oh, just sit down." Leena sighed, taking her seat one table away and waving to me. I tried not to blush, remembering how she'd used me as an advertisement for Chantara's styling services.

"What if he scares everyone off?" Kai whispered, probably to make sure the cameras didn't catch his bad attitude.

"I can hear you, you know."

People like him were why I hated this island sometimes. He acted like I terrified people on purpose, like I didn't wish I could smile and have people walk toward me instead of freezing in fear.

Kai settled into his chair reluctantly, whispering not-so-quietly to Leena, "I bet he doesn't get a single fan showing up."

Leo whirled around me, reaching his hand out to Kai. "I'll take that bet."

"Leo!" He was just as bad as Chantara, making a bet I was obviously going to lose.

"You will?" Kai's voice was laced with a smug arrogance that made me want to punch him. Except, violence would just prove he was right about me and I was somebody to fear. "Fine by me. If no fans show up to duel him, then you two have to stop dragging the duelist image through the mud and leave the Shimmering Isles."

"Not a chanc—"

"And if Damon does have fans show up," Leo trudged on, grinning his own arrogant grin, "then you and your beautiful partner have to duel us."

I rubbed my hand over my face, resigned to living my life based on bets now. It was apparently the cool thing to do. At least I couldn't be blamed when everything fell apart. I glanced at Leo's wheelchair, at his missing leg. My gut clenched. No. All of this was still my fault. It would always be my fault.

Which made it my job to get this duel. To make sure we could stay here and earn the money for an Atlantean prosthetic. No matter what I had to do, no matter what weird clothes I had to wear, I'd get that money. Leo deserved it.

"Afraid to duel us?" I asked. "Or just afraid of being wrong about everything?"

Kai frowned. "You can't really think you'll have any fans show up. This little makeover," he waved his hand at my new appearance, "isn't going to magically change who you are."

Chantara had promised me the new outfit would make me more approachable but still let me be myself. It would be amazing if the prediction came true, which made him calling Chantara's hard work a "little makeover" irritate me more than his assumption I wouldn't attract any fans.

She'd put so much effort into my new hairstyle and picking out this outfit. She'd even called the store ahead to discuss options for me, planning it out as well as she could to minimize the time I had to spend in the store feeling awkward. I had to try to make her efforts pay off.

I held my hand out. "Do we have a bet?"

Leo's eyes brightened, looking like he wanted to punch his fist in the air in excitement. I hadn't joined in on his shenanigans in a while, so he was probably happy I was playing along.

"Yes, it's a deal." Kai took my hand, dropping it as quickly as he could. He must not have wanted anyone to see him making deals with me.

Now came the hard part: hoping somebody, anybody, came to duel me.

***

Half an hour passed and nobody showed up. Kai had already finished two duels with virtual fans using holographic projection magic. He'd treated them so well I was almost fooled into thinking he was a good guy. Until their images faded away and he just shook his head at me, reminding me that our bet was still on and I wouldn't be on this island for much longer.

I pulled my phone out, debating if I should text somebody to take pity on me. That was probably cheating, but Kai hadn't specified any rules for the bet. Who could I ask? I scrolled through my contacts, most of whom didn't live on the island. I hovered over Chantara's contact. She'd said she was coming to the event, so maybe she'd be willing to do me a favor.

No. I couldn't ask her to do that. She didn't really know how to play Divine Duelist. Plus, seeing how little her styling had helped me would probably make her sad.

A group of people walking by stopped to stare at me, probably because I was glowering at them. They excitedly whispered to each other, but then continued walking to Leo's table.

Leo shrugged at me, as if to say it was no big deal. He welcomed the fans genuinely, shuffling his cards with a smile. He never had problems gaining fans, which was the only reason we'd survived on the Shimmering Isles as long as we had. It was all going to go away now because of a stupid bet.

I glanced at my phone again, at Chantara's name. She was so full of gleeful energy, I bet she could turn the mood around here. Just her being in my general vicinity would make me seem less frightening. Maybe I should message her after all.

A woman cleared her throat. "Is this seat taken?"

"Chantara?" I yelped, accidentally hitting the call button on her contact. Her phone started playing a relaxing ocean melody that put me at ease. I hung up quickly and managed a smile, grateful she'd shown up without me asking.

Kai gave her a strange look, like he couldn't believe she was talking to me. I wanted to tell him to suck it, but I took the high road and pulled out her seat, motioning for her to join me.

Her eyes glimmered like sunlight on the water as she sat down. She was wearing a shimmering dress that flowed around her like jellyfish moving through the air, drawing everyone's attention. And I mean everyone. The world seemed to stand still for a moment as everyone gazed at the beautiful water nymph sitting in front of me.

She waved hello to Leena and pulled out an Aphrodite deck that was probably one of Leena's spares. "Don't be upset if I'm awful at this."

"Upset?" I shook my head, awkwardly running a hand through my hair. "You being here is all that matters. If you're awful, then we can be awful together. It'll be fun."

People seemed to freeze again, staring at us. Had I said something bad? I glanced at Leo and he mouthed the word "smooth" but didn't seem to be mocking me. I focused on Chantara, trying to ignore everyone else as warmth spread across my face.

These stares felt different from usual. People were looking straight at me with curiosity instead of avoiding my gaze. Many even seemed... flirtatious? That couldn't be right. Those looks must have been meant for Chantara. Except, she looked a little flustered herself.

She shook her head, shuffling her deck with a smile. I followed her lead, drawing five cards. The table was spelled to play a miniature version of the game, letting our cards come to life as tiny two-inch versions of themselves.

As Chantara played her first card, seashells materialized on the table, lining her side of the playing field. She added some pearls, which draped over the shells like they were table decorations instead of defensive cards usually attached to other cards. It was a weird first play since the pearls couldn't defend her divine favor points without that attachment.

"What's wrong?" she asked, a delicate eyebrow raised as if she was calling my bluff on letting her play as bad as she wanted. "I happen to like seashells and pearls."

Of course that was why she played them. Because she liked them. Only Chantara would play a game like that, not caring about tactics or winning strategies. I couldn't help the smile tugging at my lips as I sorted through my cards to find something that sounded fun too. Ares decks weren't built for fun, but I'd try my best.

I played two torch cards, lighting up the table with their soft glow. "I'll add some mood lighting."

She grinned, obviously enjoying that I was playing along. Getting two torches in the first hand was usually pointless since they cleared the miasma left behind from my other cards being destroyed, but in this game, they'd done exactly what I'd hoped for. They made Chantara happy.

"Ohhh, this one looks fun!" She played a seduction card, her gaze flicking to me. "Think I can seduce you, dear Damon?"

Her voice was full of amusement, but it also felt like a challenge. Like she meant more than just in the game. My heartbeat pounded in my ears. Was she flirting with me? I hadn't flirted with anyone in years, not since the attack, but she really didn't seem to care how I looked. It seemed as if she... liked me.

I couldn't focus on my cards, not when her gaze was making my skin tingle. I wanted to see where this would go, but it just didn't make sense that she was sitting here, in public, with somebody who looked like me. It had to hurt her shot at becoming famous, but she didn't seem to care. I bet I could be a minotaur and she still wouldn't care as long as she was happy in my company. Which she must have been. Why else would she be here?

I picked a random card and tossed it down. A Spartan warrior rose from it, lit with the red light of the aurora as if he was covered in blood. So much for the fun atmosphere.

Chantara's face fell a bit, like she realized my mood had changed. She was too perceptive, noticing every little thing about me even when I tried to hide it. I forced a smile.

"You can seduce him." I grabbed another card, one of the few pretty cards in an Ares deck. "I'll also play a drakon."

The magnificent drakon shot up out of the card, clawing its way above the playing field to circle the sky. Drakons were guardians of the gods' sacred places, massive creatures that were almost mythical. I hadn't heard of a single human ever seeing one, so how accurate could these cards really be?

Her eyes followed its long body as it dipped and curled through the air. "It's beautiful..."

Like you.

I didn't have the heart to attack her, so I ended my turn.

After a few turns, we both had all our divine

favor points and full playing fields. We'd also drawn a crowd of fans, who watched our silly game where nobody was ever attacked.

Chantara clapped her hands as Eros, the god of love, joined the gods of desire and the avenger of unrequited love, flying above the playing field in what looked like a dance with my drakon card. The way the cards moved around each other was mesmerizing, as if they'd rehearsed the patterns of dips and spins, getting close to each other, but never touching.

I could relate. Chantara was leaning over the table, her hair falling softly around her face. I wanted to brush it back, to see that beautiful smile of hers even clearer, but I stayed where I was. Admiring her from afar was all I could do.

"I forfeit." She grinned, setting her cards down. "Thank you for such a fun game."

"Wait, you're leaving?"

My voice must have sounded anxious, because she leaned a little farther and kissed me on the cheek. "I'll stick around until the event's over."

As she sauntered away, my fingers brushed my cheek, which was still warm from her kiss. Or maybe I was blushing again. Sadly, Kai ruined the moment with a vicious whisper.

"She does not count." His voice was low.

"You need an actual fan to show up, not Leena's pity friend."

Her what? I glanced at Leena. Was she why Chantara had shown up? Leena shook her head as if to tell me she hadn't done anything, but that was hard to believe. Chantara had shown up exactly when I'd needed her most. That couldn't be a coincidence. Was that a pity kiss?

No. Chantara wasn't like that. She followed her emotions and did whatever seemed fun at the time. She'd enjoyed our duel. She'd enjoyed spending time with me. Hadn't she?

Before I could overthink it, another woman sat down. I vaguely recognized her, but I couldn't remember from where.

"Hi!" The woman's voice was full of excitement as she held her hand out to me. "I'm Darcy. I was in the salon when you were getting your hair done. It looks great! I meant to tell you then, but you kind of, well, left really fast."

Her words came out quickly, like she was afraid I might run away again if she wasn't fast enough.

"Thank you." I shook her hand, but wasn't sure what to do next. "Do you want to duel?"

She let out a breath. "Yes. Please."

This was weird, but it meant we'd won the bet. Leo was grinning from ear to ear, giving Kai a gloating look. We'd get our duel with him and stay here, but honestly, I was too concerned about the woman in front of me to care right now. Even if Chantara had been taking pity on me, which I wasn't sure about, this woman didn't know me. She'd have no reason to be here except wanting to duel me.

I had a fan. An actual fan. And there were others lining up behind her, waiting to duel me next. Was this a dream?

A glint of shimmery blue drew my gaze. Chantara was waiting for me behind the line, smiling like she knew this would happen. Like she'd had no doubt I'd have fans lined up to duel me. I guess she'd won our bet then, because the TV station had to approve of us now.

Things were finally looking up and all it had taken was for me to look like a villain. I didn't understand it, but I was happy. And so were the fans.

CHAPTER 5 – CHANTARA

Watching Damon's confused expression as more and more fans showed up to duel him was the cutest thing I'd seen in a while. This was going exactly how I'd hoped it would. Damon was so surprised by all the attention he was getting that he was just going with it. He didn't talk with anyone much, but it didn't matter.

That was the beauty of the dark and brooding look I'd given him. People didn't expect him to be a big conversationalist. So if he felt uncomfortable, he could just stay quiet and duel like he was so good at. The fans were eating it up.

His gaze often searched the crowd for me, as if wanting to reassure himself I was still here, waiting like I'd told him I would. Each time he found me, he gave me a little smile that made my heart flutter. I pulled my bottom lip into my mouth, still surprised I'd kissed him in front of all these people. I hadn't wanted to embarrass him, but I'd gotten caught up in the moment.

Being around Damon was fun. He could have destroyed me in a few turns, but instead, he'd played along, not once attacking me. Winning hadn't been his goal, making sure I had fun was. He understood the point of this fan event better than most duelists.

My mission here was done. I'd chatted up lots of duelists over the past few hours, handed out at least a dozen business cards, and Damon was doing great. With that long line of fans, this had to get the TV station off his back. Which meant I'd get him and his brother as clients, adding to my growing list of famous duelists. I'd be promoted in no time. But I had the urge to draw this bet out some more, to draw out our time together.

After most of the fans had filed out of the stadium and the cleaning crew started clearing out the tables, I walked over to Damon and Leena.

"Congratulations," I said, smiling.

Damon and his brother had amazed looks on their faces. Damon grinned, a big smile that held nothing back. "I can't believe how many people showed up. To duel me!"

"Of course they did." Leo nudged him. "You're amazing."

Damon glanced away, but caught my gaze. "No, Chantara did all the work. I just sat here."

"Oh, come on. All I did was give you a haircut and some new clothes." I tried to laugh it off, but something about the way he was looking at me—almost like he thought I was a goddess—made my stomach tighten.

Before I let Damon's appreciation get to my head, I handed the Aphrodite deck back to Leena. "Thanks for letting me borrow this."

"Anytime." She leaned in close. "What's with you and Damon? That duel looked intimate."

I bit my lip, watching Damon and his brother talk excitedly about the duels. "Intimate, huh? That could be fun, if I wasn't so focused on my job right now."

"You can be a famous hairstylist and have a life, you know." Leena shook her head like she just didn't understand where I was coming from. "Maybe he could even help you with your job. Doing things like this together wouldn't be a distraction; they'd be helpful."

"Maybe."

That was a dangerous thought. One that could end up with me thoroughly distracted right when I was about to be promoted. Unless she was right and I could put my entire self into both things at the same time. I'd tried that before, though, and it had never worked. I always felt bad putting my own dreams above somebody else's and ended up helping them at the cost of my career. Falling for an underdog couldn't happen again.

"Just think about it." Leena smiled at me then headed after Kai, who'd slunk off without a word after the event ended.

I had a feeling I'd be doing nothing but thinking about it now that she'd put the idea in my head. Spending time with Damon these past few days had been so much fun. I didn't want it to end just because of a future that might not even happen. Maybe Leena was on to something.

"Hey, Damon, do you want to grab dinner? To celebrate?"

He froze, like a small fish hiding from a predator. I wasn't that intimidating, was I? Or was he just not used to all this attention? Maybe I should let him rest after a long day of dealing with all these people instead of asking him to go out and converse even more. He seemed like he'd need time to recharge and think about what it meant for him. He was about to get a lot more attention than he'd ever had while being on the Shimmering Isles.

"Uh..." Damon glanced desperately at Leo, like he needed somebody to save him. "Sure, we'd love to celebrate."

"We?" Leo raised an eyebrow. "As much as I'd love to spend more time with you, brother, I've already got plans."

He grinned, rolling over to a pair of gorgeous women who'd been keeping close to him for most of the day. One of them grabbed the back of his wheelchair and steered him out of the arena, ignoring the fact that the wheelchair's wings would have done that just fine.

"Don't forget to stop by for your haircut, oh new client of mine," I called out to Leo, who just waved his hand like he understood, but had other things on his mind right now.

At least one brother knew how to have fun. Had Damon ever been like that before the attack? Did he go out on dates and laugh and just enjoy himself? Or had he always been shy like he was now? I had the urge to learn all about him, what he was like back then and what he liked to do now.

Was I falling for him? I glanced at him fidgeting

with his cards, his eyes darting to mine every few seconds like he wasn't sure what to say, but he seemed happy I'd asked him out. Wait, was that what I just did? No. This was a business dinner. We could talk about all sorts of hair-related things...

I groaned. That excuse was flimsy at best. I should talk to him about this, see what he was thinking. For all I knew, he didn't even like me and then I could get back to business as usual.

"C'mon." I linked my arm through his and started walking toward the restaurant.

The smile he gave me warmed me to the core. We walked in comfortable silence, just gazing up at the beautiful aurora. There really was nothing else like it. The night view on the Shimmering Isles never disappointed. Especially when you got to watch it with somebody else.

"Thank you." Damon jammed his hands into his pockets, looking away from me with a blush. "It means a lot that you came today."

"No problem. It was fun." More fun than I'd had in a while, actually, and I wanted that playful feeling we had to continue. No time like the present to see if he liked me back. I stepped in front of him and put my hand on his chest. "Think I deserve a reward?" I leaned in close, whispering in his ear. "Maybe a kiss?"

I expected him to pull away in shock, for his eyes to go wide like I'd said something scandalous, but instead, the side of his mouth quirked up in a smile.

"You're not like anyone I've ever met before." He brushed a strand of hair behind my ear and rested his large hand on my cheek. "You tease me, laugh with me, and your smile fills every dream I've had since I met you. You see beyond my scars. You see me."

I leaned into his hand, covering it with my own. "Of course I see you. You're kind and so dedicated to your brother. A bit awkward, but in an adorable way." I grinned as he looked at me in shock. "What? I've thought that ever since your bad boy image shattered when I doused you in water."

"About that..." He tilted my head up, closing the distance between us. His breath tickled my lips, his voice low. "I'm ok getting a little wet."

Then his lips were on mine, confident and strong as he kissed me with more enthusiasm than I'd expected. It was like once he knew what he wanted, he was all in, completely sure of himself. Heat coursed through me, steam curling from my entire body as he touched the small of my back, pulling me closer.

I wrapped my arms around his neck, smiling against his lips. "Damn. If that's what every kiss with you is like, we're going to have a lot of fun."

"Promise?" He kissed me softly, almost tentatively compared to his bold and sensuous kiss a moment ago. Frown lines creased his forehead and his eyes seemed to plead with me for something. Like he was afraid I was getting his hopes up for nothing.

I wanted to see more of the confidence that had peeked out for a moment. I wanted to feel more of what he'd made me feel with just one kiss. I wanted to... screw it. I wanted him. I wanted his adorable little awkward smile and his confident kisses that made my entire body tremble. I wanted all of it and more.

"I promise." I kissed him again, taking my time and enjoying it so he knew I meant every word. I let my hand wander a bit, playfully hooking his pocket to tug him closer. "This is a celebration, after all. Fun will be had."

"That's not what I mea—"

"I know." I smiled at him, hoping he could open up to me more and heal some of the wounds he'd been living with for far too long. "I want to see where this goes. With you."

The smile he gave me was so bright it was like looking into the sun. He didn't say anything else, but he wrapped his arms around me, hugging me against his chest. That was all the confirmation I needed. He wanted to see where this went too.

A different kind of warmth spread through me this time. He thought I was the one who saw him like nobody else did, but he had that backward. He looked at me like I was one of a kind, like nobody else could replace me. And that was a feeling I could get used to. Or get lost in.

If I really wanted to see whether this could work, then I had to be honest. If he knew I was prone to putting too much into one thing, either him or my job, then he could notice it when it was happening. He could even help me realize it so I could adjust before things went haywire. Because he mattered to me, but so did my dreams. There had to be a way I could have both. Maybe he'd be willing to help me like Leena thought.

Damon kissed me on the forehead, then pulled away, studying me. "What's wrong?"

"Nothing, just thinking." I turned to look at him better. His attention was focused on me, waiting for me to explain. "So, I'm sure you've noticed that I'm a bit... over the top sometimes."

He nodded, barely holding a smile back. "Maybe a bit. But I like it."

He actually liked when I was over the top? I hurried to continue before I talked myself out of this conversation and just gave everything I had to the sweet man in front of me.

"And you know how important becoming a hairstylist is to me..."

He nodded slowly, like he wasn't sure where this was going. "You really should open your own shop. I bet the TV station will approve it after the miracle you've worked on my image."

"Miracle?" I rolled my eyes, grinning. "You're the one pulling this off, not me. You did great with the fans tonight."

"We did great." His voice was soft. "So if this conversation is leading somewhere bad, just tell me."

"No, it's not like that. I just need your help with something."

His eyes widened. "You need my help? With what?"

I gripped his hand, walking again as I heard his stomach rumble. I had promised him food, not an awkward conversation.

"With keeping me on task and forgiving me if I get a bit caught up in work sometimes."

He angled us toward a small food cart on the side of the road instead of the restaurant I'd originally intended. He glanced at me, silently asking if this was all right, and then ordered two squid skewers after I nodded. I moved closer to pay, but he just shook his head and let them scan his tattoo for the money.

"Why don't we go somewhere private? The beach, maybe?" He was busy gathering our food so I couldn't tell what he was thinking. "I'd rather avoid people right now if that's ok."

I decided to let him lead the conversation. We could talk about my problems more if things between us got serious. Right now, I was fine with just having fun with him in the moment. Maybe that was the key to a work-homelife balance: not overthinking things.

"Of course." I took the skewer he offered me, the sweet smell of it filling the air. "I'm guessing today was pretty overwhelming?"

"It was fun, but I'm just not used to all those people." He bit into his squid, pausing to savor it. "We also got that duel with Kai, so your plan worked."

"What?" I almost dropped my squid. "That's amazing! How did that happen?"

He sighed. "Leo made a bet. You're rubbing off on him."

I burst out laughing, scaring a seagull into flight. Damon shook his head at me, but I just grinned and headed out to the beach. I'd barely known these brothers for a week, but I was already rubbing off on them? I couldn't wait to see how they'd be in a month.

The sound of the waves lapping against the shore was welcoming. It made me want to dive in, but I resisted. Damon had probably taken me here to talk about something, so jumping into the water would be a little abrupt. We finished our squid in comfortable silence, just enjoying the ocean on a beautiful night.

"The ocean puts you at ease, right?" He took his boots off and walked out into the water until it was up to his ankles, then turned back and held his hand out. "Come on, before a wave pulls me away."

I stared at him, bathed in the aurora's glow that was also mirrored in the surrounding water. I'd never seen somebody so strikingly handsome while also being so open and kind. His smile drew me in, leading me to the water.

Somehow, he knew I was the one overthinking things this time. All I could do was nod as I slipped off my shoes to join him. A wave crashed into me, drenching me up to my knees, the cool water taking all my troubles away in an instant.

"Now we can talk," he said. "I know it might not seem like it, but I'm not a needy person."

"I didn't say you—"

He laughed. "It's ok, I know I've been a little anxious since we met. What I'm trying to say is that if you get lost in work for a bit, I'll still be around when you have free time again. Or I'll be around for a late-night beach moment like this if you need to relax. I'll just... be around." He glanced down, a blush creeping across his face. "If you want me to be."

So that's why he'd brought me here, to show me he could help me relax. How did he even know the ocean would do that for me? Probably because I was a water nymph, but still. Nobody else I dated had ever been that thoughtful.

"Is that fair though? You won't resent me if I choose work over you sometimes?" I wiggled my toes in the sand, avoiding his gaze. It sounded horrible saying that out loud, but I needed him to know what he was getting into. "My other boyfriends did and guilted me into avoiding work. We both ended up unhappy. I don't want that for either of us."

"That won't happen." He put his arm around me, pulling me into his side. "Because I'll be just as busy as you now that everyone's seen this fancy new style of mine." He laughed, gripping my shoulder tight. "Seriously though, I understand. We'll be a team. Working when we need to work and playing when we want to play." He glanced down at me. "If that's what you want."

"I—"

"Don't answer now. Just think about it."

He wasn't an underdog like I'd initially thought.

He just hadn't found his way to shine yet. Now that he had, he was so much stronger. This could work. If we kept being open like this and honest with each other.

"This is really sweet, you know. Thanks for bringing me here." I rested my head against his shoulder, gazing out at the ocean sprawled in front of us.

He kissed my temple and stayed with me, watching the waves come in and roll out until the sun rose.

CHAPTER 6 – DAMON

Being in the salon with Chantara again felt a little awkward after my big speech a few nights ago. I'd promised I'd be around whenever she wanted me to be, but I wouldn't interfere with her job. Yet here I was, at her job. Was this ok? She'd been really busy since the fan event, but we'd texted a lot. Heck, I still felt giddy from our time on the beach. That had been everything I wanted and more.

"Damon?" Leo dragged my name out like he'd said it a few times already. "I'm getting the best haircut of my life and you're not even paying attention."

"You really need more attention?" I glanced

around the salon at the women peeking at him from every angle. They'd probably bombard him for autographs any minute now.

He just shrugged, grinning like a cat that got into the cream. I rolled my eyes, smiling as Chantara laughed at us. Having all three of us together felt, well, kind of perfect. It was nice that they got along so easily.

Chantara's deft hands snipped and trimmed Leo's hair in an artful way that was mesmerizing to watch. Even her coworkers seemed to notice as they nodded their appreciation at the color choice and the style. Leo's hair was more strawberry-blond now and had lots of layers. It seemed like she was trimming the last few bits and then she'd be done.

"Sorry I've been so busy. We've had a flood of customers lately." Her gaze caught mine in the mirror, her blue eyes as fathomless as the ocean. "I've got the day off in a few days though. Want to get together?"

Her voice was hopeful, like she was really trying to make this work. Which I appreciated, but a few days meant she'd be working during our big duel against Kai. I thought Chantara went to all of Leena's games, so why would she miss this one? If I asked about it, she'd feel guilty and try to come. Wouldn't that make me the distraction she'd been worried about?

"Of course he wants to get together." Leo grinned. "You're coming to our big match too, right? You are the reason we got it after all."

She raised an eyebrow at me. "I was kind of waiting for somebody to ask me to it..."

So she knew about it. Did that mean she was coming? My heart beat faster at the thought. She'd promised to cheer for me at my next duel. Which would be this one. I wasn't sure I'd be able to focus on the duel with her out there looking like a goddess and cheering for me with the passion and excitement she'd cheered Leena on with. Wait.

"Won't you be cheering for Leena?" I glanced away, not wanting to see her realize it would be me versus her best friend. She had to cheer for Leena; she'd known her for years.

"Nevermind," I said. "Leo, we should be practicing. We can't mess this duel up."

He sighed. "Have a little more faith in our team, brother. We'll win this. And Chantara can cheer for two people at once." He winked at her. "Right?"

"Definitely." She grinned, but it felt a little forced. "I'll just rearrange a few things and I'll be there."

"Don't worry about it." My stomach clenched. I didn't want her to rearrange things for me, no matter how much I wanted her there. "We'll catch up on your day off." I lowered my voice, leaning closer. "Take advantage of all the new customers and get that promotion you deserve. You're too good not to."

Her scissors faltered as she stared at me, not in the mirror, but straight at me. Her expression looked surprised, like I'd either said something weird or people didn't tell her to keep working very often. That's what she wanted though, right? To focus on work just as much as a relationship?

"Careful," Leo mumbled, leaning away from her scissors. "I'm all for flirting, but not at the risk of my hair."

"Sorry." Chantara blushed, focusing on Leo again while she finished the last few cuts. "All done. I noticed you like to pull it back into a ponytail, but I'd try this instead."

She twisted his hair up behind his head, kind of in a messy bun, but also kind of like a high ponytail. Whatever it was made his hair look half the length. She toyed with the front of his hair, making sure long strands fell around his face. Then she nodded, satisfied.

"What is this witchcraft?" Leo's eyes were wide as he touched his shorter hair. "I love it!"

"I'm glad."

Chantara's smile made any weird feelings I'd

had over the duel disappear. She'd taken the time to get to know Leo's usual hairstyles and found a new one he'd love even more. She thought of everything, just like she had with me. Even if I hadn't appreciated it at first.

While Leo leaned closer to the mirror, marveling at his new look with a few of the women that had been admiring him, I went over to pay for the haircut. Chantara took my wrist in her delicate hands, scanning my team tattoo that connected to my account. Her fingers curled around my wrist, gripping me tight like she wanted to reassure me that everything was ok.

"Thank you." I moved my thumb across her wrist lightly, just barely touching her beautiful blue skin.

She gave me the same playful look she'd given me right before we'd kissed, sending a shiver of excitement through me. It was a look that said she was happy to be near me. So what if she might miss one duel? There would be others.

"Anytime." Her voice was low, like she was telling me a secret. The rest of the shop faded away, as if we were the only two left here. "I'll see you soon, okay?"

I nodded, then pulled away before I got swept up in her energy and did something stupid. Like kiss her in front of all these people. My ears burned at the thought and I hurried out of the shop.

I glanced inside at Chantara laughing with her coworkers and pulling Leo's wheelchair back so he could turn around easier. Warmth and happiness radiated through the window, like everyone inside was living their best lives while I looked on from the outside.

That was how I'd felt ever since the attack. Like I was watching my life go by from the outside looking in. Chantara had been the first person to make me think I could change. With her by my side, anything felt possible.

Leo left the shop alone, which was surprising considering how many people had been admiring him. Which probably meant he wanted to talk, but about what? I hadn't done anything worth lecturing me about. Had I? When we got a few blocks away from the shop, he spun his wheelchair around in front of me, forcing me to stop walking.

"What the heck was that?" He gave me one of his you've got to be kidding looks. "You ran out of that shop like your hair was on fire. And what was with you pretending not to care if she comes to our duel? It's all you've been talking about for days, but you apparently hadn't even asked her to come yet?"

My brother had never had crippling social anxiety, so he wouldn't understand. If I asked her, then she'd feel obligated to come, which could count as a distraction, which might make her rethink being with me, which would ruin our entire future. It was just easier not to bring it up. I almost laughed. That sounded a little ridiculous, even to me.

"It's nothing. Let's just go home."

He crossed his arms, like he had no intention of moving until I told him everything. Leo was so annoying when he thought he should know something.

"Things are fine." I sighed, wishing we could talk this out at home instead of on the street where I'd be mortally embarrassed if a camera caught this on film. "She just wants to focus on her job. I respect that."

He frowned. "So she doesn't want to date anyone then? She seemed pretty flirty for a woman who wasn't interested..."

"Well," I ran my hand through my hair, looking for cameras. "She didn't say she wasn't interested. She just said she needs some space sometimes, to focus on work so she doesn't get distracted."

"Giving somebody space and not telling them important things are completely different." Leo shook his head like I was being dense. "If you fit together as well as I think you do, you won't be a distraction. You'll be her strength."

"Right. Like I could be anyone's strength."

I laughed painfully and walked around him, determined to get home before the conversation got worse. "Besides, we shouldn't be distracted right now either. We have a duel to win. A duel that could change our lives."

If we won, we'd finally start rising in the ranks and earning real money, money that could buy the best Atlantean prosthetic leg we could find. I'd be damned if I screwed up my best opportunity to help Leo. He'd lost his dreams because of me once. I wouldn't let it happen again.

Leo grabbed my arm, yanking me back. "No way. You don't get to just walk off like it's not important." The wings on the back of his chair were flung out to catch up to me. "You're being ridiculous. There's a beautiful, amazing woman back at that shop who likes you, and you're acting like it doesn't matter."

"Of course it matters!" I shrugged him off. "But what if getting close to me messes everything up for her?" I motioned at his missing leg for emphasis. "You more than anyone else should worry about that."

"Me more than anyone else?" His words were low, full of a fury I hadn't often heard from him. "And why is that?"

Was he really going to make me say it? "You

know why."

"No, I really don't. Enlighten me."

I glanced around, once again wishing we were alone instead of in the middle of a busy street downtown. A few people stopped to stare at us. Why was he doing this now? He was being difficult for no reason. But I could tell he wouldn't let me leave without finishing this conversation. So I had to say it. Had to admit my biggest failure in front of who knew how many people.

"Because I'm the reason you can't walk."

Guilt washed over me like a tidal wave. He couldn't get up and go for a run or sweep his girlfriend off her feet or climb the tree outside our house to sneak inside after curfew or anything else that came to mind. I'd taken his life away from him. All because I was bored and wanted to explore somewhere we never should have been.

I turned away. I couldn't even look at him right now. He meant everything to me and I'd put him in danger. I'd failed him when he needed me the most. How could I even think about getting into a relationship? My fingers clenched around one of my daggers. If I'd had these back then, if I'd known how to use them, maybe things would be different now. Maybe I could have fought off the chimera better, given the adventurers more time to get to us. Maybe—

"Stop." Leo hadn't moved, but something in his voice made me turn around. His eyebrows were pinched together. "You have to stop this before the guilt swallows you whole." He inched closer, like he was a hunter trying not to scare a deer away. "What happened to me wasn't your fault. If you want somebody to blame, blame the chimera."

"Well, yeah, but—"

"But nothing." His voice was firm. "You don't get to keep blaming yourself for something that wasn't your fault. I'm honestly pretty tired of it. You saved my life." He nudged his wheelchair into my legs. "Are you listening? You. Saved. My. Life."

"The adventurers did that."

After I'd put his life at risk. I hadn't known a chimera would be there, but I was still the one who'd dragged him out that day. Into an unknown area, seeking an escape from my boring life. I'd give anything to be boring again if it meant he still had his leg.

Leo sighed. "You're such an idiot."

"What?"

"You heard me." He shook his head, like he couldn't believe how dense I was. "Those scars you're so ashamed of are proof that you fought tooth and nail, literally, to save me. You did everything you could. You threw yourself between me and a terrifying monster to make sure I survived. Sure, I lost a leg, but I could have lost my life. I'm happy to be alive, so you need to forgive yourself and move on with your own life." His voice lowered to a whisper. "Don't let that day haunt you forever. You're allowed to be happy too."

Was it really that simple? Just forgive myself and move on? He was right—I had done everything I could to save him. And we'd both gotten out of there alive. But he would never be the same. My scars just made me ugly; his injuries meant he couldn't walk.

"Don't you blame me? Even a little?"

I'd never managed to ask him that, no matter how often I'd wondered about it. He tried so hard to be cheerful, to make sure I didn't feel bad about anything, that he'd never given himself time to get angry about it. To scream at the world for how unfair it was. To yell at me for talking him out of that date to keep me company instead.

"Still an idiot." Leo laughed.

"How can you laugh at a time like this?"

"Because you're being ridiculous. If you want me to blame you, I can." He cleared his throat like he was preparing for a big speech. "Damon, I blame you for being awesome and protecting me.

Oh, wait, that's a good thing. Hmmm... I blame you for spending all your time dueling so I can get that expensive Atlantean leg I've been eying up. No, still a good thing." He tapped his chin. "Wait, I blame you for even considering ruining a perfectly good shot at love. Yeah, that's a crime right there."

"Shut up," I mumbled, but a smile crept across my face. Leo was always like that, finding the good in every situation. "Be serious for once."

"I've never been more serious." He held my stare, daring me to look away. "I just can't find anything to actually blame you for. I never could. I'm grateful for what you did and that's it. Accept it or stay miserable forever."

Could he be telling the truth? He really didn't blame me? I wasn't sure I could say the same if our places were switched, but he was always the better person in that way. If he truly meant it, if he didn't blame me, then maybe it was time I stopped beating myself up. I hadn't intentionally hurt him; I'd never do that. Sometimes life just sucked, but at least we were alive to live it.

I hung back to follow him so he wouldn't see the tears welling in my eyes.

"Well, if those are my only choices, I guess I'll go with acceptance."

Leo sighed, falling back into his wheelchair

like he was exhausted. "It's about damn time."

Had my guilt really been bothering him that much? I'd have to do better from now on, making sure my emotions didn't burden him. If he was happy, then I wanted him to stay that way. He was the best brother I could ask for.

I ruffled his newly perfect hair. Maybe if I messed it up enough, we'd have to go see Chantara again to fix it. Or I could just go ask her to come to our duel, remind her that she was supposed to be cheering enthusiastically for me. Try to let myself be happy without guilt nagging at me. There wasn't anybody I'd rather try to be happy with.

CHAPTER 7 – CHANTARA

Getting fans hyped for Damon's upcoming duel against Kai required eye-catching posts showcasing the dark and sexy villain versus the golden boy hero. Half of the promos were much easier to make than the other—or, at least, much more fun. I knew it was good for publicity and that I'd come up with the idea, but showcasing Kai as a great hero kind of made me sick.

"Leena?" I called over to where she was reorganizing her deck on the couch. "You're a bit deluded by Kai's greatness. Care to hype him up as some great hero so I don't scream at my computer?"

She frowned. "Well, when you put it like that, how can I refuse?"

"Sorry, you know what I mean."

I sighed, happy to not look at any more pictures of Kai as I scrolled through ones of Damon instead, who was much easier on the eyes. The only pictures of his new style were from the last fan event, but they all looked good. Which ones would the fans like best? The ones where he had a tiny little smile? Or maybe the ones where he looked like he wanted to murder somebody?

A shiver ran through me as I scrolled past one of those. The intensity in his gaze had me thinking about that first kiss. About how in control he'd been, how strong.

"What's up with Mr. Tall, Dark, and Handsome anyway?" Leena leaned over my shoulder, murmuring her appreciation for the picture. "You've been oddly tight-lipped about it. Usually when you like somebody you overshare. A lot."

"I do not!"

Leena snorted. "Come on. You've described some guys in such detail that I can't even look them in the eyes later."

"True." I tried not to smile, because half the reason I overshared was to see her reactions. I enjoyed having somebody I could talk to about anything. "Ok, so here's the deal. We kissed—"

"What?"

I winced. "I know, I should have told you sooner. But it was pretty magical. So magical, actually, that I got a little worried I'd fall head over heels for him."

"So you've got what everyone wants; no need to brag about it." Leena laughed, but froze when I frowned. "Unless you don't want him?"

"No, I do." Yesterday at work, my entire body had screamed at me to kiss him right there in front of all my coworkers. I would have enjoyed it too, but it wasn't the best way to prove to my boss that she could trust me with a promotion.

I hadn't known Damon long, but everything in me wanted to spend more time with him. I wanted to be the first one he let behind that wall of his and break it down with a tidal wave. He was always so kind, trusting me even when it made him uncomfortable. It was like he knew I'd never hurt him, that I had his best interests at heart. I wanted to repay his faith in me.

"But it's not that simple." I dropped my head onto my hands on the table. "I've wanted to be a hairstylist for years and I'm so close. But I also really like Damon and think we could have a future together."

I'd never thought of any kind of future besides becoming a hairstylist. Beyond that was just too hard to grasp, like mist over a lake. But Damon had me dreaming of more. This could be a real relationship if I let it.

"You still don't think you can handle both?" she asked, looking at me like this whole conversation was ridiculous. "Just don't go overboard on either and find a good balance. You'd be living the dream, having a job you love and a guy who likes you just as much as you like him."

"Have you met me? When do I not go overboard?" I raised my eyebrows at her. "Remember when I took the whole month off to help my sister rebuild her sandcastle adventure business after her partner dropped out?"

Leena groaned. "That business was doomed to fail. Or what about that merman you hooked up with who expected you to help him fish trash out of the ocean all day?"

"Hey, that was a good cause, and our ocean never looked cleaner." I slumped against my chair, remembering how I'd gotten fired for being late too many times because of that. "What if Damon's just another person who needs my help? I was supposed to be breaking the pattern, not falling back into it."

"I guess so..." Leena bit her lip as she

manipulated an image of Kai into the ad I'd been making. She put light behind him like he was some kind of sun god. Ugh. Good thing she was doing it instead of me.

"So that's that then." I sighed, sinking even lower in my chair. "You were supposed to talk me over to your side, not start agreeing with me."

She stopped manipulating the picture to focus on me. "Sorry. But you do realize Damon's different, right? His goals line up perfectly with yours, so anything you guys do will help both of you instead of just him."

"How so?"

"He wants to be a great duelist, which requires a great stylist." Leena winked. "And you want to be a great hairstylist, which requires great duelists to show off your new styles. If you work together, you'll be unstoppable. The perfect team."

The perfect team, huh? I hadn't thought about it like that before, but she was right. It was the whole reason I'd set up our bets in the first place. I just hadn't thought about it in terms of romance. He wouldn't distract me because we both wanted the same thing, to be great at our jobs.

Leena said duelists needed great stylists, but just changing his hair hadn't been what really helped Damon. It was a new haircut along with a new outfit. Hmm... that was an idea we should try out: partnering with Rhapso, who'd bring clothing options to the salon so duelists could get complete makeovers when they came for their haircuts.

"You look like you're overthinking this."

I glanced at Leena, who looked worried.

"No, you actually just gave me a great idea." I shook my head as her eyes lit up with curiosity. "Nope. I have to run it by Damon first."

I'd need his help, so it was only fair to talk with him first. He'd be the perfect spokesperson for my new idea.

Leena sighed. "Fine. Then at least tell me about that date of yours after the fan event."

"We had dinner at the beach and he promised to take me back there whenever life got overwhelming." I smiled just thinking about it. "It was pretty sweet."

"Jealous!" Leena joked. "Guys like that are hard to find. Better hold on to him."

I focused on the picture of him I was editing, on the expression in his eyes. No matter how terrifying I made him look on the outside, he was a big softie on the inside. He'd been so careful not to admit how much he hated the haircut I'd given him to avoid hurting my feelings. He'd also agreed to that hot outfit just because he thought I liked it, even though his face was red with embarrassment.

If I let myself like him, let myself really see where things could go between us, I knew we'd be happy. I could just feel it. We respected and wanted what was best for each other. I'd never had that in a relationship before and I really wanted to give it a try. To give him a try.

"Guess I should think of a costume to wear to this duel then." I bit my lip as a grin stretched across my face. Letting myself like somebody again felt good. "And ask somebody to switch shifts with me that night."

"That's the spirit!" Leena grinned, smacking me on the shoulder. "You can fall in love with him and still get your dream job."

In love? Was I already falling in love with him? No, that would be crazy. I busied myself with putting shadows behind Damon's picture to contrast the light she'd added to Kai's, trying not to focus too much on his face. Every time I looked at him, even a picture of him, my stomach flipped like I was a teenager with a crush.

"Now the real question is, who are you cheering for tomorrow?" Leena's grin was full of mischief, like she'd realized something I hadn't. "You do realize cheering for him means you're cheering for my enemy, right?"

My eyes widened. I always cheered for Leena, no matter who she was dueling. I'd planned on cheering for them both, but what if she was offended?

She laughed, motioning with her hands for me to calm down. "I'm just kidding. I'll survive one duel with you cheering for the other team."

"Probably for the best." I'd told Damon I'd cheer extra ridiculously if I went to one of his duels. "You'd be embarrassed by me, honestly. I'm going to be a bit over the top."

"How is that different from usual?"

"Shut up." I laughed, nudging the computer at her. "Let's finish these up and post them. I want everyone watching this duel. The TV station will have to keep Damon here after this."

Which meant I'd get to spend more time with him. I pulled out my phone, messaging him about grabbing dinner after the duel. Dots showed up like he was replying, then disappeared, then came back, and disappeared again.

Eventually he replied, "Can't wait."

Two simple words had my heart pounding. Yes, giving in to my feelings was the right decision. It had to be.

CHAPTER 8 – DAMON

Our duel against Kai and Leena was about to start, but instead of focusing on that, I was standing here, checking my phone every two minutes. Chantara had asked me to dinner, but hadn't said anything else. Was she going to break the news that her job was too important to risk? Or was this a date?

Ugh. The unknown really freaked me out.

"Damon?" Leo asked. "I think you should take a look around."

"Sorry, I know I'm distracted. I just wish—"

Chantara was in the stands, using her water magic to spell my name like she'd done for Leena the day we'd met. My name shimmered in the air as she directed the water through the crowd. She wore a dark jacket and were those daggers? I squinted. That was definitely not the kind of outfit she usually wore.

Leo started cackling. "Gods, she's cosplaying as you! She's amazing."

"What?"

Sure enough, she'd even styled her hair to hang off to the side like mine. It was absolutely ridiculous, just like she'd promised it would be. My heart pounded in my ears. This had to be a good sign, right? That she was here, openly supporting me, must mean she'd asked me out on a date. Not just a friendly breakup dinner.

"You look worried." Leo wiped his eyes like he'd been laughing so hard he'd cried. "Still wondering about that text from her?"

"It's gotta be a date, right?"

I should just ask her. I could clear this all up with one simple text. But what if it wasn't a date?

I shuffled my deck as Kai and Leena entered the arena. I had to focus. This duel would change everything for us. We were finally on the big stage, prime-time television. If we played this right, we'd be matched in better duels from now on. We'd make way more money too.

But my eyes kept wandering to Chantara. To how her body moved as she spun around, weaving her water magic like the movements of the drakon in the game we'd played. She was beautiful. And she was here supporting me. That meant more to me than she'd ever realize.

"Let's hurry so I can—"

"Go on your date?" Leo scoffed, drawing his hand of cards. "What kind of guy cares more about a date than a duel?"

"You, actually." I rolled my eyes at him, but I enjoyed how relaxed this duel felt. I'd assumed my entire body would be in knots over the stress, but one look at Chantara and it all just melted away. "So just play awesome and let's win this."

He grinned. "That's what I like to hear. We've got this!"

I played Enyo, the goddess of war, and the hounds of Ares. The dogs rose from their cards and just kept rising until they were almost up to the Enyo card's shoulders. The beasts were massive, oozing an aura of intimidation across the field.

Kai played Paris of Troy and a spell card that transformed my goddess of war into a seashell. That was less than ideal, but somehow, in this moment, it didn't even worry me. Leo and I were going to win. We were a better team than Kai and Leena could ever hope to be because we actually wanted to help each other. Kai just wanted to help himself.

The duel seemed to go by in a haze, as if I were on autopilot just waiting for it to be done so I could talk to Chantara. Her voice carried across the field, cheering me on like she was right beside me, whispering in my ear. I had to tell her how I felt. Now that I'd found somebody as incredible as her, there was no way I was backing down.

Leo wanted me to move on and enjoy my life. The best way I could do that was with her.

Drakons and flying gods filled the air while warriors covered the ground. It was a battle for the ages, but none of it mattered. The only thing that mattered was the gorgeous woman in the stands who drew my gaze like a moth to a flame, giving me all the confidence I could ever need to win. Eventually, our Spartans overpowered their defenses, destroying the last of their divine favor points.

The duel was over. Which meant I could find Chantara.

"Good luck!" Leo called out as I raced away. "Don't do anything I wouldn't do."

"Pretty short list, don't you think?" I laughed, making my way to the stands.

Unfortunately, they were full of people. People who wanted to talk to me. To shake my hand.

To hug me. It was all so overwhelming that I felt myself shrinking, like if I got small enough, I'd disappear and they'd all go away. I was happy we had fans now, but this was so strange. People kept congratulating me and smiling at me and all the sorts of things that usually happened to Leo.

It was like I was popular now too. I shuddered. That would take some getting used to.

Chantara slipped between a few fans, smiling at me. "Looks like you need a rescue."

She grabbed my hand and took off running. I had no choice but to follow her as we darted around enthusiastic fans who I should have been talking to and thanking for coming. But I could save that for another day. A day when Chantara's fingers weren't curled around mine. When she wasn't grinning at me slyly like she had some mischievous thing planned.

I was beginning to like mischievous things. If they were planned by her, at least.

Instead of going to a restaurant as I'd assumed we would, she led me to a small glass igloo. At the entrance, she paused, like she was suddenly uncomfortable.

"I made us dinner." She gave my hand a tiny squeeze. "Unless you'd rather go somewhere else?"

"This is perfect." I tentatively kissed her on the

cheek, but my face was burning so hot I bet she could feel it. "Thank you."

She smiled and tugged my hand, leading me into her home. The glass walls were tinted in shades of blue with jellyfish lights hanging from the ceiling and pearls strung up like streamers. The floor was the color of sand, giving the whole place a peaceful underwater vibe that fit Chantara perfectly. Not to mention the giant pool in the middle, where food was laid out on floating tables.

"Is that where we're eating?"

I wasn't the best swimmer, but the pool didn't look deep. I shouldn't really complain when she'd gone to all the trouble of making dinner too.

The sound of fabric shifting drew my attention as Chantara dropped the jacket she'd been wearing. It pooled around her feet, revealing a sheer dress over a white bikini. The dress clung to every curve of her body like it was made specifically for her.

"Only if you want to." She stepped into the water and my gaze trailed up her legs, over her hips, and to her chest, where the water lapped against her skin like it was welcoming her. I'd never been that jealous of water before in my life. "Or I could move the food somewhere else."

"No." I shook my head quickly. "This is more than fine."

I took off my coat, setting it down by hers, but then didn't know what to do. I didn't have a swimsuit and I definitely wasn't ready to be naked in front of her. Leaving her all alone in the water felt rude though. Especially when she looked that good...

"I got you a swimsuit. Thought it might be easier." Chantara shrugged, like planning out our entire date down to my clothing was totally normal. "It's on the chair."

She nodded across the room. I picked up the black-and-red swim trunks, once again having no idea what to do. I could be bold and just take my pants off, but that made me panic just thinking about it.

"I'll cover my eyes if it helps." Chantara's laugh was warm as she covered her eyes, then split her fingers apart to peek.

"Really?" I raised an eyebrow at her and she laughed again.

"I was only kidding." She turned around to do something with the food, giving me the privacy I needed to change. "I got a T-shirt too in case you didn't want your scars showing. Honestly, I really don't think they're a big deal, though. You should be proud of them."

My fingers hovered over the shirt I'd been about to put on for that very reason. She'd known exactly what to do to make me comfortable. When had she gotten to know me so well? Or was she just that kind of person?

I walked back to the pool, shirtless. If she was ok with my scars, then I had no reason to hide them anymore. They were part of me and I needed to accept that. I took a step into the water, which was warmer than I'd expected.

"So no shirt then, huh?" She smiled like it made her incredibly happy I'd chosen that option and slid closer to me. She delicately traced one of my scars with her fingers, as if she was afraid of scaring me off. "I hope you never feel the need to hide around me."

"Same to you." I put my hand on hers over my heart. "I know you thought we'd distract each other, but I think it's in a good way. Seeing you at my duel lit a fire in me. It's why we won so easily."

"Oh?" She leaned forward, lightly kissing me on the lips. "Guess I'm your lucky charm then."

She was far more than that. She was the light leading me to the surface of the water I'd been drowning in. She was the hope of a future better than I'd ever dreamed. She was... everything to me.

I ran my fingers lightly along the back of her hand, up her arm, enjoying the look on her face as I reached her neck. She moved closer, titling her head like she was inviting me to touch more. To feel more. I bent down, kissing behind her ear as I let my fingers slide down her spine. Her hair smelled like coconut as I trailed kisses down her neck.

A tiny moan escaped her lips as she put her hands on my shoulders, arching back a bit into my hands. Her breasts pressed against my chest, and a smile danced on her lips. My heartbeat thundered in my ears at that look, at the desire in her eyes. She wanted me just as much as I wanted her.

I pressed my lips against hers, pulling her into a kiss that made my head spin. Her arms slid behind my neck, linking us together as if telling me there was no escape now. This feeling in my chest wasn't just attraction, it was more than that. It was bigger than anything I'd felt before. It was pure and strong and happy. Just like her.

"Well," she gasped as she pulled away, "that was unexpected." She kissed my lips one more time then pushed off my chest to swim toward the table of food. "But definitely welcome."

She was grinning like she wanted to play, like that was an invitation to follow her. I obliged, swimming closer to her as she ate a grape.

"You're not worried about distractions anymore?"

I shouldn't have asked, but I had to know. I'd need to slow down and think things through if there was any possibility she might change her mind about this.

Thankfully, she just grinned even more. "Nope."

"Thank the gods." I sighed, grabbing a grape and letting my hand brush against hers. "What changed your mind?"

"Leena, actually." She treaded water, a thoughtful look on her face. "She helped me realize our goals work great together. I can keep helping you please your fans and you'll keep helping me become a better hairstylist."

"So you're just using me?" I raised my eyebrows at her, then laughed. "No, it makes sense. I'm on board."

Especially since it meant being with her. It was nice having somebody on my side, battling the fans with me. Well, I had Leo too, but that just wasn't the same.

"Good. I actually have a favor to ask you." She paused. "I was thinking about asking my boss to make a deal with Rhapso. To have clothing stylists and hairstylists work together for full makeover appointments when duelists need a refresh."

"Now that's a good idea. It would have been so much faster to do both those things at once." I gripped the table floating between us. "Except, I wouldn't have gotten to spend all that time with you then."

She rolled her eyes like I was being cheesy, but tiny curls of steam rolled off her cheeks. "So you'll help? Talk to her about it with me? Since you went through the whole makeover process and all."

Her eyes were focused on the food on the table instead of me, like asking this was awkward for her somehow. Or like she didn't think I'd say yes. Why would I refuse such a simple thing that could help her?

I pushed the table, sending it floating away from us, and pulled her into my arms. Her eyes widened.

"I'll gladly help," I said, "but you should talk to the TV station about it, not your boss. It's an amazing idea. I bet they'd let you open that salon you wanted."

She blinked, frowned, then opened her mouth and shut it, like she didn't know what to say. I couldn't help but smile at her reaction. She was so good at what she did and was dedicated to her career, but she didn't see what was right in front of her.

"You're too good to keep working for somebody else." I leaned down, whispering in her ear, "And I'll help however I can."

"We'd be a team then?" She bit her lip. "You'd be willing to rave about me to the TV station, about how much your makeover changed your life?"

"I'd tell the whole world if it helped."

"It might." She wrapped her legs around my waist, as if she was anchoring herself to me so she didn't float away. "But just the TV station is fine for now."

"We can go tomorrow or whenever you want."

She ran her fingers through my hair, ruffling it like she was planning on styling it right now. My whole body was pulsing, extremely aware of every part of her that touched me. Like my skin was attuned to her, reacting to her every move.

"Wow, I didn't even have to use my secret weapon on you." Her eyes shone with mischief.

"Secret weapon?" Chuckling, I kissed her shoulder. "And what exactly is that?"

She leaned back to grab something from the table behind her, pushing herself harder against me in the process. Did she realize how difficult it was to concentrate in this position?

"I play seduction!" Her voice was dramatic as she held one of Aphrodite's cards in front of me like a talisman. She waited a moment while I stared at her in shock. "Well? Did I seduce you this time?"

"That's still not how those cards work." I laughed, holding her tighter as she grinned. "But yes, you seduced me the moment I met you."

This woman was silly and amazing and perfect for me. She was just so full of happiness that it overflowed onto me. And I wanted nothing more than to bask in that joy with her. To have a life full of laughter and smiles like the one she was giving me now.

I kissed her again, letting the whole world fall away as I explored her body. I wanted to know everything about her, to learn every way I could make her happy. She deserved it and I was eager to spend however long it took to satisfy her. I had a feeling I'd enjoy it too.

EPILOGUE – CHANTARA
Six months later

"Just a little farther," I told Damon as I led him, blindfolded, through the streets. "Ok, we're here."

I slid his blindfold off, watching carefully to see his reaction. He blinked, then focused on the nondescript two-story building in front of us.

"Isn't this a media company or something?" he asked. "Are we doing an interview?"

"No." I tried to stay calm, to contain my excitement, but it bubbled up anyway as I grinned. "This is a hair salon. Or it will be with some renovations."

"A hair salon, huh?" He wrapped his arms around me, hugging me from behind as we gazed at the building together. "Anyone's I know?"

I leaned back, resting my head on his chest. "It's mine."

"You really did it." He smiled against my cheek. "That's amazing!"

It really was. I'd never had something that was all mine. That I could run and manage by myself. It was everything I'd ever wanted, but it meant more now that Damon was with me.

"I couldn't have done this without you." I gripped his arm at my chest; the embrace made me feel safe and comfortable. "Leena used to joke about me opening my own salon, but it seemed out of reach. I didn't think it was possible until you became my client, and Leo too, and everything just started taking off." I turned my head so I could look at him. "You never let me doubt myself, reassuring me at every turn that I could really do this. You made this possible."

"Just like you made my dream possible. Your creative styling helped us earn enough money to buy Leo's new Atlantean leg." Damon leaned in closer, his lips against my ear as he whispered, "I love you."

A smile crept over my face. I turned around, kissing him hard and fast like a sneak attack. He laughed.

"I love you too." I kissed him again, slower,

enjoying the moment with him. "Want to go inside?" I nodded at the shop and gave him a suggestive grin. "It's empty, just waiting to be explored."

"Sure." He started to follow me, but then he swept me up in his arms and carried me instead. "But I might be a little distracted."

"Only a little?" I grinned, sliding my hands up his chest. "I might need to change that."

The look he gave me was full of heat and adoration, like I was everything he'd ever dreamed of, just as he was my new dream. Life on the Shimmering Isles was about to get a whole lot more fun.

Thanks for reading *Winning you Over*! If you enjoyed it, or hated it, please consider leaving a review. Honest reviews help readers find the books they'll enjoy and avoid ones they'll dislike. No matter how long or short your review is, it's valuable. Thank you.

Don't miss the next book in the series!

Playing
with
Lightning

She's desperate to win. He's a deity with a lousy job. When they join forces in the ultimate combat card game, will love get in their way of victory?

Leena lives for the win. Prepared to battle alongside her best friend in a globally televised magical tournament, she's left alone and betrayed when he drops her to compete with a more popular player. With her fandom dwindling as she hunts for another teammate, she risks it all by pairing up with a handsome stranger wielding a surprisingly dangerous deck.

Agon refuses to spend eternity as Zeus's enforcer. Determined to get fired by throwing the world's hottest competition, the kind-hearted godling happily joins a girl tumbling down the rankings. But despite his best efforts to crash and burn, he's shocked when his incredible partner single-handedly starts raking in the wins for the underdog team.

As Leena's bold new playstyle sends her popularity soaring, her determination to prove her skills threatens to trample her growing feelings for Agon. And while their winning streak endangers Agon's plan, he fears helping Leena in her quest means losing her forever.

Can these two defeat their opponents and still win a future together?

Pandora Pierce writes fantasy romance novels that combine all her favorite things: gaming, Greek mythology, and comedic romances. You won't find many sugary love confessions in her stories or the slaying of any mythological beasts; she loves animals too much for that. But you will find heartfelt stories with swoon-worthy couples that'll make you smile.

When she's not writing, Pandora enjoys playing board and video games, watching anime, reading, and streaming on her VTuber channels. Stories and games connect people in magical ways and she wants to share that experience with you. Join Pandora's adventures below!

Discord: https://discord.gg/jAZzTrSc5z
Facebook: https://www.facebook.com/pandorapierceauthor
Instagram: https://www.instagram.com/pandorapierceauthor/
TikTok: https://www.tiktok.com/@pandorapierceauthor
Twitch: https://www.twitch.tv/pandorapierceauthor
Website: https://pandorapierce.com/
YouTube: https://www.youtube.com/@pandorapierceauthor